*"They went to h*___ said, *"and they k*___ ___ ___ *guard on duty there."*

The man's eyes never lost their conviction. "No. My brothers would never do that."

"They did."

The prisoner's voice thickened. "No. We are sworn. Sworn to protect lives. We destroy demons; we are not life-takers like you. Our missions are sanctioned by our deity, made clear by the training we are provided, made holy by our prayers."

"You drove a truck through the wall of a diner."

"There are things in this world and in others that a mortal and even immortal mind cannot know," the man responded.

Angel saw the conviction in the madman's gaze. *He believes what he's saying.*

"She's your death come walking," the man promised hoarsely, trying to hold Angel's gaze even as the trustee slapped a pair of cuffs on him, locking his hands behind his back. "You can't trust her."

Angel™

Angel: City Of
Angel: Not Forgotten
Angel: Redemption

Available from POCKET PULSE

ANGEL

redemption

Mel Odom

**An original novel based on the television series
created by Joss Whedon & David Greenwalt**

POCKET PULSE

New York · London · Toronto · Sydney · Singapore

Historian's Note: This story takes place during the first season.

An *Original* Publication of POCKET BOOKS

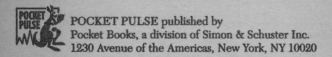

POCKET PULSE published by
Pocket Books, a division of Simon & Schuster Inc.
1230 Avenue of the Americas, New York, NY 10020

ISBN: 0-671-04146-0

First Pocket Pulse printing June 2000

10 9 8 7 6 5 4 3 2 1

Printed in the U.S.A.

To Lisa Clancy, for the friendship and professionalism, and for believing. You make this work fun and exciting.

Acknowledgments

To my son, Shiloh, who simply wanted to see his name in an *Angel* book because he thinks it's a good show. (He wants to learn the David Do-Wop Dance!)

To Dr. Gary Wade, friend and optometrist, who keeps me working in spite of the endurance marathons I put my eyes through.

To Drs. Donna and Brian Johnson, who take care of the whole family.

And to Coach Eddie Gossman, for building memories for the eleven-to-twelve-year-old Tar Heels football, basketball, and baseball teams.

ANGEL

redemption

PROLOGUE

Goose bumps suddenly covered the back of Whitney Tyler's neck. It was a feeling she'd gotten before, one she recognized from other times when she'd been spied on by a half-dozen stalkers and thousands of fans. The cool air blowing from the air-conditioning vents inside the Mitsubishi 3000 GT suddenly felt positively glacial.

Cars, trucks, and vans on either side of her sports car jockeyed for position on the L.A. freeway. Whitney wondered if the uneasy feeling had been caused by one of the nearby drivers suddenly recognizing her as Honor Blaze, her television series alter ego.

She had a tendency to draw attention, she knew. She stood five feet ten inches tall in her stocking feet and had red-gold hair that spilled past her shoulders. She wore the Honor Blaze look: black leather pants, platform sandals, and a dark magenta knit top that showed off her figure. The black duster that pulled the look all together lay in the passenger seat.

Whitney put on her left turn signal, checked the traffic, and flowed into the next lane. Taillights flared ruby flames in front of her without warning, and she had to step hard on the brakes to avoid a fender-bender. Breathing rapidly, she glanced in the rearview mirror and watched as the SUV behind her shrilled to a matching pace less than a foot away.

The driver laid on the horn angrily, and the sound filled the car.

"What's that?" Gunnar Schend demanded at the other end of the cell phone she held. He was the producer of the Honor Blaze series.

"I cut a guy off changing lanes. He was honking to show me the new Uzi he got for Christmas."

"Hint: not laughing. Ergo: not funny."

Whitney checked the traffic around her, peering into the dark car interiors sporadically illuminated by dashboard lights and the cars following too close. When she glanced into the rearview mirror, she saw a big wrecker truck suddenly cut in front of the SUV that had dropped back behind her. The huge hook at the back of the wrecker swung violently from side to side as it closed on her.

Whitney spotted a break in the traffic on her right. She put her foot down hard on the accelerator, and the fuel-injected engine pushed her back into the seat.

Even as she pulled into the other lane, she saw the wrecker change lanes behind her, having to fit in behind an older full-sized sedan. The hook at the back swung wildly.

"Whitney?" Schend called.

"Someone's following me." Whitney kept both hands locked on the steering wheel.

Without warning, the wrecker surged past the sedan, pulled in front of it, and rammed the Mitsubishi's rear.

The sports car briefly skidded out of control, crossing halfway into the lane to the left. Whitney pulled hard on the wheel, narrowly avoiding colliding with an RV decked out in orange running lights and an illuminated picture of Elvis across the back.

"Whitney!" Schend called.

"He rammed the car!" She glanced in the rearview mirror and saw the wrecker gaining speed again. Her taillights reflected from the mud-splattered chrome bumper.

She cursed, something she seldom did, and put her foot down on the accelerator as she steered to the right and pulled onto the shoulder. She laid on the horn frantically, trying to breathe even though it felt as if her lungs were squeezing shut.

The wrecker followed her, roaring up again and slamming against her. The Mitsubishi rolled awkwardly and slewed across the shoulder, butting up against a pickup and caroming off. Whitney struggled to keep control. The sports car slammed against the guardrail and threw up a cloud of sparks against the passenger window as metal ground on metal.

She turned onto the next exit ramp, not even knowing for sure where she was. The sports car wobbled as it slewed around.

The wrecker remained in her rearview mirror, rocking on two wheels as it made the turn. One of the headlights had broken from the impacts, giving the vehicle a cyclopean appearance.

Only popping static came over the cell phone. Whitney didn't know if Schend had disconnected or the phone had been damaged. She put her foot on the accelerator again, streaking for the fluorescent oasis of the truck stop and diner at the end of the off-ramp.

Whitney ignored the stop sign posted at the end of the off-ramp. She skidded onto the highway, drawing a blast of compressed indignation and anger from a passing eighteen-wheeler that just managed to change lanes and miss her.

Lights flooded the Mitsubishi's interior without warning. Whitney glanced up just before the wrecker smashed into the side of the car. The seat belt restraint tightened between her breasts as the wrecker pushed the sports car into the oncoming lane.

Whitney cut the wheel hard left and floored the accelerator. The car ripped away from the wrecker, and she steered toward the truck stop again. She watched in frozen horror as the wrecker overtook her, coming up rapidly on the side. The smashed grille hung loose, dragging along the concrete and spewing sparks.

Whitney held on to the steering wheel tightly. In the darkness gathered in the wrecker's cab, only the driver's silhouette was visible. The man seemed huge, deep chested with a large head.

As soon as the wrecker pulled abreast of the sports car, still fifty yards or more from the diner, the driver yanked fiercely on the wheel and slammed into Whitney. Her car lost traction and slid across the concrete till it hit the curbing protecting the fueling area from the diner's parking lot. The wheels on her car's passenger side caught against the curbing, stopping her. But the momentum flipped the car on its side.

Belted into her seat, Whitney watched as the view through her cracked windshield revolved.

She glanced through the rear window and saw the wrecker coming around in a wide loop, setting up to take another run at her. She clawed at the seatbelt release and fell against the top of her car. Desperately she slithered across the cramped interior and through the broken passenger window.

She stumbled toward the diner. Several men lined the huge plate-glass windows in front of her, staring in disbelief as the wrecker bore down on the overturned car.

Whitney was through the diner's front door by the time the *crunch!* of the impact overtook her. She didn't slow, certain the wrecker wouldn't stop.

In the next heartbeat the diner's front exploded in flying glass and broken wood shrapnel as the wrecker smashed the crushed Mitsubishi through ahead of it. The car and wrecker came halfway into the diner, ripping up the tiled floor, flattening tables and chairs, and knocking people from in front of it like tenpins.

A chair slid across the floor and tangled with Whitney's feet, knocking her to the ground. She banged her chin hard enough to make her arms and legs go rubbery. She rolled over and watched the wrecker door screech open.

The driver dropped to the debris-strewn floor. He stood over six feet and looked almost half as wide. Handmade black clothes lent him a regal air. His unlined face looked young, but the hate in his volcanic blue eyes was old. His blond hair hung to his shoulders.

He carried a wooden stake in his right hand.

Whitney struggled to get up, forced her way to her feet in creaking inches. Just as she started to put one foot in front of the other, the big man seized her by one shoulder and flattened her against the wall near the pay phone. He placed all his weight against her.

He drew the wooden stake back, preparing to drive it through her heart.

Whitney couldn't defend herself, couldn't even scream. She lifted her hands, knowing he could hammer the stake through them like they weren't even there.

"It's time to go," he said. "Evil won't be tolerated. I will show you the Light."

A young trucker lunged from the whirling dust and black smoke now filling the diner. He grabbed the man in black's right wrist and succeeded in deflecting the blow to the wall beside Whitney's face. The stake sank inches into the wall, and the impact knocked the pay phone loose.

Shrugging almost effortlessly, the man in black backhanded the young trucker hard enough to lift him from his feet. He reached for the stake again, holding Whitney without strain as she tried to kick free and pull his hand from her shoulder.

A leather-clad biker stepped up behind the man in black. The biker swung a long, steel tire tool like Mark McGuire swinging for the fences, hitting the man in black behind the knee.

Bone broke with a dulled thump. The man in black collapsed, still yanking at the stake embedded in the wall. His grip on Whitney loosened only marginally.

The biker rammed the tire tool up under the man in black's chin, pressing hard against his throat to keep him in place. "Not another move, Clyde." He glanced at the CHP officer just getting to his feet with his pistol in hand. "You gonna take care of this, or do I gotta gift wrap it for you, too?"

"Make no mistake, son," the officer said, pointing his weapon at the man in black, "I'll shoot you dead if I have to."

Reluctantly the man in black rolled over.

The officer looked at the biker and held up the handcuffs. "Know how to use these?"

The biker grinned. "Used to play with my daddy's all the time."

"Make 'em tight." The officer threw the handcuffs over, and the biker cinched them onto the man in black's wrists. Keeping his weapon aimed, the officer lifted the radio mike from his shirt and quickly called the situation in. When he was finished, he looked Whitney over carefully. "Why'd he come at you like that?"

"He thinks I'm a vampire," Whitney croaked. "But I'm not. I just play one on TV."

CHAPTER ONE

"Man, this is so lame," Doyle said.

Drawn from the dark thoughts that often claimed so much of his attention, Angel glanced over at his companions. They were at a booth in Winkle's, a sports pub only a few blocks from the office.

The bar was wedged between a pawnshop and a Chinese laundry that ran a gambling book in the back. Most of the bar's clientele used Winkle's as a waystation, a place to spend part of their occasional winnings or part with some of the money they'd gotten from items hocked at the pawnshop on the way to the laundry to pay off their latest debts.

The standard in Winkle's tended toward self-service. The few hostesses used their wait positions to advertise and barter other skills that couldn't be found in the Classifieds. It was seedy and dark, the smoke-stained windows hardly letting any of the light in from the street. Where other taverns sold atmosphere, Winkle's sold pauses between desperation and panic attacks.

Dark haired and lovely, Cordelia Chase sat to Angel's right on the inside of the tavern booth on the business section of the newspaper because she'd refused to sit on the aged and scarred vinyl without some kind of protection.

She wore designer jeans and a dark blue jacket over a white crop-top that showed off the bronze tan and belly. She was in chic mode, waiting to get noticed by any producers slumming in L.A.'s dives. A copy of *Variety* lay open before her like an altar.

"It's not lame," Cordelia said irritably. "Sitting in a sleazy bar waiting for vampires to show up is kind of—well, kind of—"

"Actually, it does beat sitting at home in a crummy little apartment watching the wallpaper peel." Alan Francis Doyle sipped on his beer, then noticed the warning scowl Cordelia gave him. He put a hand over his heart. "It was my own crummy little apartment I was speaking of there, Cordelia. Not yours."

Cordelia didn't let up on the scowl.

Realizing he'd committed yet another *faux pas*, Doyle hurried on, almost choking as he swallowed and tried to speak at the same time. "I don't mean to say that your apartment is crummy. *Avant-garde*, now there's a term I would use." He tried to look earnest. Blessed with Irish charm and boyish good looks despite the mean streets Doyle's life had taken him through, the earnest look was an easy one for him to pull off.

Of course, Angel mused, *if the recipient of that look knows it's only one of several Doyle can pull off, it kind of loses its zing.*

Cordelia smiled, a little. "Do you even really know what *avant garde* means?"

"Of course I do," Doyle returned defensively.

"*Avant garde* is French. You know, one of the romance languages."

Doyle nodded enthusiastically. "Exactly. Just like Gaelic."

"Gaelic isn't a romance language."

"Then," Doyle said, grinning, "might I suggest you've never enjoyed the true pleasures of the language."

Cordelia counted languages off on her fingers. "French, Spanish, Portuguese, Italian, and Russian; those are the five romance languages."

"Russian isn't a romance language." Doyle's black hair looked as if he'd raked his fingers through it to straighten it a couple hours ago and made his sallow complexion stand out even more.

His green eyes shone in the darkness gathered in the bar. He wore dark slacks and a checked green shirt with a rumpled collar. At the moment his half-Brachen demon heritage didn't show at all. "The only thing the Russians have ever been romantic about is vodka."

"Kind of like the Irish have been romantic about Scotch," Cordelia quipped.

"Now, there's a mistake you should never make again," Doyle said. "A true Irishman doesn't drink Scotch. He drinks a good Bushmills or Jameson. See, the Scottish dry their malts over an open peat fire, which gives it that smoky taste that hangs in the back of the throat that you just can't get rid of. The Irish, being sophisticated and naturally more intelligent, dry their malts in closed kilns, making for that smooth, natural flavor that's so magical."

Cordelia rolled her eyes.

"Irish monks in the sixth century took themselves off on a little trip to the Middle East thinking they were going to learn how to distill perfumes," Doyle said. "Instead, they came back with the recipe for good Irish sipping whiskey. They called it *Uisce Beatha*, the Water of Life."

"Guys," Angel said quietly, interrupting the sometimes seemingly endless argument that went on between the two of them. They were his partners in the investigation agency he currently operated, and his friends. But there were days—well, mostly nights—when even he was hard-pressed to put up with them.

Cordelia and Doyle glanced at him. "What?" they said together.

"We're supposed to be keeping a low profile here," Angel explained patiently.

Cordelia looked around. "Actress though I may be, even I couldn't go this low."

Back in her Sunnydale days, Angel knew, Cordelia Chase's family had lived in a moneyed cocoon. She'd never known want until her father had lost the family wealth to the IRS. Once the social background was gone, Cordy had migrated to L.A., hoping to find her future in Hollywood. Working at the investigation agency was generally the only thing keeping the wolf from her door these days.

"You know," Angel said quietly, "I really could handle this alone." Besides being tall and broad shouldered, he was a vampire with more than two hundred and fifty years on the clock. There wasn't much he hadn't seen and had to deal with, and tonight's planned excursion wasn't that threatening. Dressed in a black turtleneck and slacks, wearing a black trenchcoat, he seemed like one of the shadows in Winkle's come to life.

"No," Cordelia insisted. "We're a team. We think as a team, act as a team, and slay as a team."

"Kind of a Musketeers thing," Doyle agreed.

"Meaning that neither of you have anything else to do tonight except hang out with me and wait to see if the vampires show up."

Doyle nodded and spun the bottle on the table. "Absolutely nothing."

"I'm here to soak up the atmosphere," Cordelia objected. "Rumor has it Tarantino may be trying to put a *noir* anthology together for HBO. Only with aliens. Kind of a *Pulp Fiction* meets *Star Wars* thing. I'm going to try to do a reading. It all takes place in this space bar called Rick's."

Doyle put on a gruff accent. "Play it, Sam. You played it for her, so you can play it for me."

Cordelia looked at him. "Hello? Like, from what planet did you just drop in from?"

"Rick Blaine," Doyle explained. "The owner of Rick's? From *Casablanca?*"

"*Casablanca* was okay," Cordelia said. "But we're talking a futuristic *Cheers* concept. Only with guns and mayhem added. I'm reading for a hostess role."

"Like Carla was at *Cheers*," Doyle said.

"I'm thinking more along the lines of Jessica Rabbit. They've got to let her sing, right?"

Angel and Doyle swapped looks. Sometimes Cordelia's leaps of logic defied gravity.

"Of course," Doyle answered, switching subjects. "The lame reference I was making was to this place's selection of viewing media." He raised his voice. "Hey, Wally."

The mountain of a man tending bar looked at Doyle. The dim light shone from his shaved head. "What?"

"I thought this was a sports pub," Doyle replied. "Shouldn't there be a game on? I come in here thinking maybe I might get to see some sports on TV. Kind of what drew me to the place. That, and its rustic charm, of course. You know, the Kings and the Lakers are still playing."

"You got money on a game?" Wally asked.

"Yes."

"Which one?"

Doyle hesitated. "Both."

"For or against?"

"For."

"On both?"

Doyle nodded.

"They'll never beat the point spread, Doyle," Wally replied, opening a couple bottles and handing them to a hostess. "You're going to lose your shirt."

"To the Chinese laundry?" Cordelia asked with a smile. "How charming."

"So what about the TV, man?" Doyle called back to the bartender.

Wally shook his head. "Not on Tuesday nights at this time. Tuesday nights belong to Honor Blaze."

"Where is she?" Doyle asked. "Maybe a small wager might open the whole sports world up to her."

Wally pointed. "On the screen, mate. And if you don't keep your yap shut, I'm going to have to throw you out again."

Angel had to smile at the sudden discomfiture Doyle showed. Watching the half-demon in a social scramble was a true spectator sport.

Two young men clad in jeans and Gap shirts entered the bar. Angel watched them, quickly deciding that they neither acted nor smelled like vampires.

"Honor Blaze," Cordelia repeated, flipping through the *Variety* issue. "There was an article in here about her. Ah, here it is." She marked her place with her finger, making sure the title still showed. "'In this reviewer's opinion *Dark Midnight* is absolutely the sleekest and most stylistic series of the new television season."

"*Dark Midnight,*" Doyle echoed. "Like there's ever any other kind?"

Cordelia kept reading. "With cutting-edge stories laced with human drama and tragedy, a pace that zips along with the unforgiving staccato blasts of a terrorist's machine pistol—"

Doyle groaned.

"—*Dark Midnight* starring Whitney Tyler brings a whole new verve and flair to her role as Honor Blaze, vampire shock jock of the L.A. radio scene."

That caught Doyle's attention. "Did you say vampire?"

Cordelia leafed through the trade paper again. "I wonder if she has a *grr* face. And where does she get off acting like a vampire? Of all the actresses in Hollywood, I've got more experience with bloodsuckers than any of them." Catching herself, she looked up at Angel. "Sorry."

"It's okay," Angel replied. "No offense taken." Suddenly aware of the silence that had descended over the bar, amazed that it could get any quieter, he looked around, noticing that everyone's attention was on the three television sets.

The show opened up with a scene in a radio booth. The camera panned up from stylish pumps, along slender calves and up to rounded thighs before a miniskirt's hem cut off the view. The woman's voice was soft, smoky, and sexy, the kind Angel knew had an effect on most men. And a few vampires.

"Wow," Doyle said. "Now, that's my kind of DJ."

"Quiet!" someone ordered.

The camera continued to move around the radio booth, giving the viewer a glimpse of the sound engineer working with the DJ. The guy was in his early twenties and obviously enraptured by the woman he watched through the plate-glass window.

Despite the mission he was on, Angel found his attention wandering, trying to peer through the shadows in the radio booth to get a look at the woman. Still, the camera held back, offering only hints at what she looked like. Low lights sparked fire from her red hair.

"Tonight," the DJ said, "we're talking about fringe religious groups and how much latitude they have here in America. Several listeners have called in, wanting to discuss the topic, and I have some views myself I'd like to share."

"Hi, Honor," an elderly woman's voice said. "I just had to call in and tell you that some religions that society seems to shun these days can be really supportive. After my husband died, I was terribly alone. I tried new hobbies, new friends, the whole smorgasbord of self-help concepts that are floating around out there now. But none of them worked for me. Then I met someone who invited me into their coven."

"A witch's coven?" the DJ asked. The camera panned in on her smile just above the radio mike. It was full-lipped and attractive.

"Yes, a witch's coven," the elderly caller went on.

"I've found it so fascinating. There's so much to learn, so much to understand. And I'm feeling better than I have in years. However, my children have disowned me."

"Because you're a witch?"

The elderly caller laughed. "Oh, they called me that for years, back when their father was alive. I was the authority figure, you see, since their father was gone so often."

"So their leaving you alone was no real surprise."

"They never really cared about anything other than their father's money anyway. I just wanted you to know where I stood on the subject. People just need to be a little more tolerant of things they don't understand. It seems like the faster we're headed for the next millennium, the more society's attitudes shift hard to the right. And I'm talking about the actual millennium, not the year 2000 that most folks made such a big hullabaloo about because of that Y2K thing."

"Thanks for sharing that with us, caller," the DJ said.

The second caller's voice belonged to a teen. He whispered frantically. "Help me!"

The camera panned to gray-green eyes that narrowed in consternation. "What's wrong?"

"They've got me."

"Who has you?" the DJ asked.

"The clinic." The boy at the other end cried in shuddering breaths. "I don't know the name of it. My parents put me in here for deprogramming because of some of the websites I was cruising on the Internet. Two guys I know—I'm not even really friends with them—were busted for beating up a few kids at school. They put two of them in the hospital. But I didn't have anything to do with that. They said I did, but I didn't."

"Take a deep breath," the DJ instructed calmly. "How can I help you?"

"I need to get out of here," the boy said. "My parents overreacted. They signed me in here, but they don't know what the clinic is really doing. They don't—"

A garbled scream, like someone yelling with a hand over the speaker's mouth, ripped across the phone line into the sound booth.

The DJ's eyes cut to the sound engineer. "Do you know where that call is coming from?"

"Yeah. Caller ID picked it up."

Blubbering, wheezing breath filled the phone connection again. "Damn kid bit me," a man's gruff voice announced.

"Help me, Honor!" the boy yelled.

Then the phone connection broke.

"Okay," Cordelia said. "Well, that was intense."

Doyle nodded in agreement.

Angel stared at the screen as the teaser ended and the show switched to the opening montage. Techno-pop provided a driving backbeat behind the images of Honor Blaze.

Exploding cars, buildings, and a helicopter showed between flashes of Honor Blaze battling guys with guns, knives, swords, and even a bazooka. The guys were dressed in Italian suits, military uniforms, gangbanger colors, and even what looked like nothing at all.

The techno-pop soundtrack hammered to a final crescendo as the camera panned in on Honor Blaze. She stood on a rooftop, turned away from the camera, dressed in tight-fitting dark gray Capri pants, stiletto heels, an electric blue turtleneck, and a charcoal gray leather jacket. Something ignited in the background, sending up a spray of colorful fireworks. She turned as the fireworks died away, a daring look in her eyes and a self-confident smile on her lips.

"What?" Cordelia exclaimed when the show cut to commercial. "No *grr* face? No hint even of fangs? What kind of show is this? It's obvious these people need someone with some real insight into the vampire mind." She crossed her arms. "Someone like me."

Angel stared through the television screen,

chilled even past the temperature his body usually stayed at. He felt as if someone had walked over his grave—again. He didn't know what the commercial was, barely registered Doyle's plaintive cry to the bartender for a little mercy and a quick glimpse at ESPN for the game scores.

"Angel?" Cordelia reached for him.

But Angel was drawn back into memory, following the face that had lighted up the television screen. The last time he'd thought he'd seen it had been more than two hundred years ago.

CHAPTER TWO

Galway Bay, Ireland, 1758

"Please, gentle sir, please let me up. I beg you. I know not how to swim."

Angelus held the old man by the ankle in one hand, leaning far out over the ship's railing so his victim's long hair dragged through the moon-kissed waves of the incoming tide. With his vampiric strength, holding the old man this way for long moments had proven no problem. And Angelus was strong, fresh drunk from the kegs of Irish whiskey below and from the blood of one of the women passengers aboard ship.

"You made a mistake," Angelus crowed proudly. "Two, in actuality. I am neither a gentle sir, nor do I care about your welfare, old man." He dunked the old man into the water, submerging him nearly to mid-chest even when the ship crested each wave. Sailcloth from the twin masts of the rumrunner's racing boat cracked overhead, filled by the easterly breeze that rolled in from the North Atlantic Ocean and into Galway Bay.

Cries for mercy came from the other passengers who had been taken prisoner. They stood huddled together in front of the forecastle, the light from the pair of whale-oil lanterns hanging in the rigging turning their despairing faces waxy yellow.

Angelus ignored them all, holding the flailing old man under water for a long ten-count.

"You monster!" Running footsteps, too light to be those of a man full-grown, slapped against the wooden deck.

Further amused, Angelus turned with the uncanny speed he possessed after having drunk his fill, keeping the old man hanging over the ship's side.

The dark-haired girl rushing at him was the old man's daughter. Although she was fair where her father was severe, the resemblance between them remained undeniable. She raked at him with her nails, trying to score his face. Angelus dodged out of the way easily, then backhanded her, breaking her nose and sending her flying from her feet.

"Child," a woman's voice called out, "you won't touch this man unless he allows it."

Darla stood near the railing above the forecastle, her blond hair swirling in the wind. She looked as if she'd stepped off the king's ballroom in a red, off-the-shoulder dress. Though she was petite, the hostages drew back in horror. They'd already seen her at work and feared her.

"Let my father go," the girl ordered, her lower face a mask of blood. "He has nothing to do with the Scottish or the rebellion they are fomenting against the English crown."

"Of course." Angelus released the hold he had on the old man's ankle, dropping him at once into the deep, natural harbor of Galway Bay. He smiled good-naturedly.

The old man screamed, but it was short-lived, ending as soon as he submerged.

"Father!" The girl staggered to the railing, crying out in sorrow and horror.

"Don't fret, girl." Angelus grinned. "It's a long way to Galway shore or even the coast of Ireland. Maybe he'll learn to swim. And tonight, the tide does favor him."

Her shoulders shook as she cried out helplessly, and before Angelus could stop her even with his great speed, she hurled herself overboard.

Angelus stared down into the dark water. For a moment he saw the girl, limned in the white blouse she wore, the water so black the material looked as blue as coal dust. Then she disappeared.

The women among the hostages began crying and wailing.

It became readily apparent that the girl couldn't swim, either, because she never came up. The absurdity of her decision to die with her father appeared as ridiculous to Angelus as a nightshirt on a milk cow. High on blood and alcohol, the vampire threw back his head and roared with laughter.

Angelus bounded up the stairs leading to the forecastle deck. Lightning flashed again, setting the black sky afire for a moment, and a hard rain fell in a torrent. The storm had been threatening all day.

"Having fun?" Darla asked.

"More than is humanly possible," he assured her.

"I understand about playing with your food," Darla said. "Any vampire would. Blood is just so much more intoxicating with adrenaline flooding it. But I was talking about your adventure here, getting to play pirate."

"I've always wanted to be a pirate." Angelus sheathed the cutlass through the wide crimson sash at his waist. Except for the sash, all his other clothing was black, including the knee-high boots. "Looting and pillaging has been agreeable. All that's missing is a mysterious map that leads to buried treasure."

Darla pouted and touched his face. "Is this a more enjoyable time than any of those I've shown you?"

Angelus took her into his arms and swung her about. "Never, never have I ever felt more alive than when I'm with you."

"Life," Darla said knowingly, "is such a dreary existence. It's much better to be undead."

"Yes," Angelus agreed. He was still new enough to the vampiric life that his references tended to the mortal rather than the immortal mindset.

The sleek cargo ship was called *Lugh's Fancy,* named after her owner, a smuggler who ran between England and Ireland on a regular basis. Darius, the vampire sea captain they'd only recently had the occasion to meet, had come to Angelus with the plan to overtake the vessel and use it for transport to their main target tonight. Angelus hadn't been as exuberant as Darius, but his ties to Ireland weren't the same as those of Darius.

Lugh Kirevane's current run to Galway had been to drop a shipment of muskets to the Galway militias that were being formed to suppress the remnants of the Scottish Rebellion. The unrest had also served to stir up the old grievances against the Catholics.

Under Darius's cunning leadership, the band of

vampires had taken *Fancy* when the vessel had put in at a hidden harbor only a few miles south of Galway. Darius had led the brief but furious battle that had left the shore teams dead, then orchestrated the ship's capture when Kirevane dropped anchor.

Now they were after far larger prey.

"There she is!" a man called from the rigging above.

Angelus looked up, spotting the man high in the rigging. He was a vampire, an ex-sailor as was all of Darius's crew.

"Where away, Mr. Roberts?" Darius roared from the ship's stern, where he handled the big wheel himself.

"North by northwest, Cap'n," Roberts called back from the rigging. "We're a-headed right for her."

Excitement flared anew through Angelus. He took Darla by the hand. "C'mon."

"Where?" she asked, following reluctantly.

"To Darius. I want to watch him steer the ship." Angelus scampered down the steps in spite of the rain sluicing across the deck. His coat billowed around him, catching the wind as he sprinted up the steps to the stern forecastle.

Darius Lynch was big, topping six feet by a handful of inches and carrying over two hundred and fifty pounds spread across a broad frame made heavy with muscle from working as a shipwright and blacksmith when he'd been human. He gripped the handles on the great wheel, legs spread as he used his body weight to steer *Fancy* as the wind sent her racing across the choppy water. He wore a great beard filled with iron-gray hair, matching the unruly locks that fell from under the kerchief wrapped around his head. He'd been sired late in his mortal life.

An oil lantern hung from the navigator's table next to the ship's wheel. As it swung, the lantern sent crazy shadows leaping across the deck and railing. "Ah, Angelus, me fine young friend. And be ye having a great time of it, laddie?"

"The best," Angelus replied enthusiastically as he peered into the darkness, striving to see the other ship they'd been searching for. Lightning seared the sky again, and he spotted a dark, triangular shape upon the sea. "How can you tell one ship from another so far away in the darkness?"

Darius laughed; he'd been hitting the whiskey pretty hard himself since they'd found it among the cargo. "Ye're not a sailing man, lad, else ye'd never ask that. A man what lives upon the sea, he knows more of her mysteries and of them what bides time upon her than any landlubber ever could." He nodded. "That's *Handsome Jack*, all right. I'd wager me right arm on it."

Driven before the wind, *Fancy* closed rapidly on the other ship.

"They're a-having to tack into the same wind what's pushing us. Even if they was to try to run from us now, ol' *Fancy's* quick enough to catch them." Darius bellowed orders to his crew, commanding them to change some of the sails. "And tighten them up snug, you no-good layabouts. I won't have them sails luffing."

Angelus's stomach tightened in anticipation. Staring across the storm-tossed seas, narrowing his eyes against the strobing lightning flashes, he saw the bobbing lanterns aboard the other ship. He wore his demon's face proudly, knowing it would strike terror in the hearts of those he was about to meet.

A few minutes later the vampire in the rigging called down, "They've seen us, Cap'n."

Concerned, Angelus watched as *Handsome Jack* suddenly came about, reversing direction. The other ship's sails filled almost instantly, pale white quarter moons ballooning against the black night.

"They're making for the coastline," the vampire lookout called down.

Angelus turned to Darius. "Will they get away?"

Darius grinned. "Let 'em run, lad. I always enjoy the chase. And no, they ain't a-going to get away. I'll promise ye that. Taking a ship at sea is a mite trickier than what we did to get ol' *Fancy* here, but me and these men have taken a few ships in our time. This one will be no different, I'll warrant."

Standing at the stern railing, Angelus watched as *Fancy* closed the distance on *Handsome Jack*.

They were less than a hundred yards out when *Handsome Jack*'s crew fired a cannon shot across *Fancy*'s bow. The sudden bloom of orange fire exploding from the smaller ship's deck marked the cannon's position.

Angelus heard the heavy hiss of the cannonball pass by only a few feet over his head to splay in the bay, followed immediately by the sound of detonation. Sound traveled more quickly over water than it did over land, but it didn't travel as quickly as the flash of light.

"Either they got a good marksman aboard," Darius said, "or that was a lucky shot." He raised his voice, never flinching from his chosen course. "Run out them guns, you scoundrels."

Amidships became a flurry of activity as Darius's crew pulled the heavy, protective tarp from *Fancy*'s four sixteen-pound cannon. They rolled them over to the starboard side on the heavy iron-cast wheels. Care was taken with the gunpowder barrel the vampires used to charge the cannon. They rammed sixteen-pound cannonballs down the enormous throats.

"Are ye prepared to fire?" Darius demanded.

"Aye, sir!" a chorus of yells replied.

"On my signal then, you terrible excuses for true fighting men."

Running full out now, *Fancy* crested the waves often instead of her prow slicing through them. When her forward momentum was spent, the ship slammed back down against the water with jarring force.

Angelus turned to Darius. "Isn't all this battering hard on the ship?"

The old ship's captain laughed. "Ah, lad, ye are a pip. This old girl can take all these seas have to give her and more. Grab ahold of that cutlass and wave it about like ye be a proper pirate."

Angelus slid the cutlass free and peered across the dark water, seeing the haggard and nervous faces of the men crowding *Handsome Jack*'s deck. A few of them tied lanterns up in the rigging, throwing more light over the sea. Farther ahead of them, the dark coast of western Ireland could be seen.

Waves slapped against both ships as they sped across the water, and the sound was caught between them, echoing and intermingling with the shouts of the men on both vessels. Another cannon aboard *Handsome Jack* fired, spitting orange and yellow flames. The *whumph!* of the cannon going off sounded a heartbeat later.

This time the cannonball slammed into *Fancy* and sent a palsied shiver through her that echoed through the deck under Angelus's feet. Anxiously he peered down at the ship's side, trying to find the spot where they'd been hit.

"They didn't hole us, lad!" Darius cried out. "When that happens, the crack of timbers shattering rings out instead of that great bloody boom ye just heard."

Angelus glanced at Darla, but her smooth countenance gave away nothing. He looked back at *Handsome Jack,* now less than sixty yards away. Two crews worked at the cannon, dumping powder and balls into them. But another group of men surged onto the deck with muskets. They shouldered their weapons and fired, covering that part of the deck for a moment in thick, roiling black smoke.

Shot rattled against *Fancy* like hail. One of the hostages went down screaming in pain. A hole appeared in the canvas near Angelus's head.

"Steady on, lads," Darius commanded. "Keep yer powder dry." *Fancy* closed the distance to forty yards and fell in beside *Handsome Jack*. "Leave off sail, ye great muttonheads! Match our speeds!"

Darius's crew brought some of the canvas sheets down, and Angelus immediately felt the change in *Fancy* as she slowed. They came alongside the other vessel easily.

"Gunners!" Darius bellowed. "Mark ye well yer targets! I want them two masts shivered!"

Peering across the distance, Angelus saw two men dressed in finery. Evidently they were part of the king's men, as Darius had promised.

"Be careful when you board," Darla quietly warned beside him. She touched his face again, softly.

Angelus glanced at her, knowing she was aware that he made his own decisions. "Why?"

"I have a feeling that there is more to this ship than even Darius knows." Worry shone in her eyes.

Angelus grinned and shook his head. "Nothing's going to happen to me. There's not a man living who can harm me."

"Gunners," Darius bellowed, "fire!"

The sudden thunder from the cannon ripped across *Fancy*, drowning out even the ragged screams of the wounded hostage. Even as he reeled under the auditory assault, Angelus watched as *Handsome Jack*'s rear mast suddenly shattered a few feet above the deck and twisted violently in the rigging.

The sails furled uselessly, whipping about in the wind without capturing it. Another cannonball scattered the men on deck, hammering some of them flat and knocking two of them over the back railing.

The carnage fired the dark hunger that ruled Angelus's thoughts. He gripped the cutlass more fiercely. "When do we take the ship?" he asked Darius impatiently.

"Now!" the old captain replied. "Ready yer grappling lines, boys, we're a-gonna bring this here fish in!"

Fancy pulled to within thirty feet of *Handsome Jack* when the first casts were made. The grappling hooks spanned the distance easily, bit into the ship's railing, then the vampire crew hauled with all their savage strength, pulling the two ships together and tying off the lines.

Handsome Jack's crew grabbed hand axes and tried to slash the grappling lines, but the vampires swarmed across the distance, making the jump easily, and battered the human sailors back.

Unable to restrain his own blood fever any longer, Angelus hurled himself across to the other ship. He landed on the deck, confronted immediately by a burly pirate who swung a hand ax at his head. Angelus dodged back, a cruel smile on his lips.

Angelus reached for the sailor's arm and twisted it. Bone snapped sharply, and the man screamed in pain. In the next instant Angelus slashed his throat with his nails. The vampire drank the rich, warm blood as he watched Darius's crew rip through the humans.

Darla landed only a few feet away, her face marked by the hunger that rode her. She snarled at the sailor before her. The human swung his ax at her head, but she reached up, blocked the swing, then ripped out his throat with her other hand.

"Grab the wheel afore we break up on them rocks!" Darius stood upon *Handsome Jack*'s deck now, battling ferociously with one of the well-dressed men who had an honest gift for swordplay. "If this ship goes down while we're tied up, it's liable to drag *Fancy* down as well."

Dropping the corpse he held, Angelus peered ahead of *Handsome Jack* and spotted the jagged rock fangs above the waves less than a hundred yards distant. The ship was headed straight for them.

Angelus ran toward the ship's stern as the rain continued to pound down from the dark heavens. Two others of Darius's crew ran with him. He raced up the steps, dodging the hanging tangle of ship's rigging and collapsed sails. Then he was at the great wheel.

A long sliver of wood from the ship's deck or the broken mast jutted out of the helmsman's chest. The dead man's glassy eyes stared into the dark sky, mirroring the lightning crackle that flashed above.

Angelus yanked the corpse away and grabbed the wheel. He couldn't see through the fallen sails to where the broken rocks speared up from the waves, but he thought he remembered. He pulled hard to the left.

Handsome Jack smacked up hard against *Fancy*, nearly knocking Angelus from his feet. He hung on stubbornly but couldn't help laughing at the absurdity of the situation. They'd come there to catch *Handsome Jack;* now it looked as if the other ship had caught them.

"Let me at that wheel, lad," a vampire pirate ordered gruffly as he waved the fallen sail away. "We—" A look of surprise suddenly filled his scarred face. He glanced down at the wooden sliver that jutted through the center of his chest, piercing his dead heart. In the next instant his flesh disintegrated, leaving only his skeleton behind. Even before the rack of bones could fall, they exploded into dust as well. The roaring wind whipped the dust away.

A figure stepped through the shadows created by the flailing sails. She was decidedly feminine, her curves showing through the black breeches and bell-sleeved white blouse she wore. There was no fear on her face as she lifted the metal-sheathed wooden rapier she carried into the en garde position.

She was beautiful, Angelus realized, and he felt drawn to her even as he wanted to slap the confident smile from her face. She had her red-gold hair pulled back, letting it run down her shoulders.

"Come on, you godless creature," the young woman challenged as she set herself on the pitching deck. She pulled one arm behind her in a fencing stance. "Let's see if I can find that narrow spot where your soul once resided!"

Without warning, she came at him, the wooden sword leaping for Angelus's heart with unerring precision.

CHAPTER THREE

"Angel?"

Angel stirred restlessly from the hypnotic pull of the memory, noticing Cordelia was staring at him as if expecting an answer. "I'm sorry. Did you say something?"

"Obviously nothing you were interested in." Cordelia gave him her miffed look and returned her attention to the *Variety* paper.

"I'm interested," Angel said. "It's just that Whitney Tyler reminded me of someone I met . . . a long time ago."

"Anyone we know?" Cordelia asked.

Angel hesitated. "No. This was a *long* time ago."

"As in, before the invention of the automobile?"

"Yes."

Cordelia shrugged. "Ancient history."

Angel felt uncomfortable. Memory of the young

woman aboard *Handsome Jack* was one of many he no longer wanted to remember. That young woman and hundreds like her were reasons he was in L.A. now. "Right. Nothing interesting."

Cordelia gave him a high-wattage grin and her full attention again. "Oh, and do I sense dish in the offing? An old, unrequited love? A secret tryst?" She made a sour face. "Or someone you put the bite on back before you got reunited with your soul and now regret?"

Angel blinked. Even after all these years Cordelia's lack of social graces could surprise him at times. She prided herself on telling it like it was, even if she sometimes missed the big picture.

"Just be warned," Cordelia went on, "if this is one of the maudlin, self-recriminating, poor-me-I-used-to-be-such-an-evil-vampire moments, I'm really not interested."

Still, there was something vaguely secure about Cordelia's lack of tact. It seemed eternal, something that could always be counted on.

"That whole act," Cordelia said, "is just too entirely much like the maudlin, self-recriminating, poor-me-I-never-wanted-to-be-the-Slayer mantras I used to have to put up with from Buffy. I mean, you were what you were, and you are what you are, and you'll be what you'll be."

Doyle shook his head. "My, and aren't you

Martha Stewart and Dr. Spock all wrapped into one tonight."

"Life is what you make it," Cordelia stated. She glanced at Angel. "Even unlife."

Angel returned his attention to the television screen. Whitney Tyler, as Honor Blaze, was back in action. The resemblance between her and the young woman on *Handsome Jack* was nothing short of uncanny. He watched her, mesmerized.

"Well?" Cordelia said.

Angel glanced at her. "Well what?"

"What kind of moment were you having? You can't just leave us hanging like that."

Angel nodded. "It was one of those maudlin, self-recriminating, poor-me-I-used-to-be-such-an-evil-vampire moments."

"Not interested." Cordelia glanced through the trade paper some more.

Doyle excused himself, went to the bar, and returned with two fresh bottles of beer. He handed one to Angel.

Angel glanced at the label. "Switching from the imported stuff?"

Doyle shrugged and gestured to a small TV behind the bar. "The Kings just got drilled in the third period, and the Laker Girls are looking better than the Lakers in the fourth quarter." He uncapped the bottle. "I'm just hoping that permanent press is the only absolute over at the Chinese laundry, you know?" He lifted the bottle in a silent toast. "To your health."

"And a change in fortune." Angel put his beer on the table, not really intending to touch it again.

Doyle watched the large-screen television. "This show is not such a bad idea. Maybe you should consider talking to someone in the industry yourself. Sell them your story. Bad vampire regains soul, finds love, loses girl, sets out to redeem himself from all the evil he's done by taking on evil. I'm guessing at the very least we're talking about a Movie of the Week deal here."

Cordelia folded the paper, excitement glowing in her dark eyes. "You need to let me handle this."

Doyle gave her a sidelong glance. "You? I'm the one who thought of it."

"Yes, but I'm the one with the Hollywood connections." Cordelia leaned into the table, as if afraid someone around them might overhear. "You know, this could really work. Look at how popular Anne Rice and all her vampire novels are. Not to mention all the money involved. Of course, we'd have to lose the whole detective shtick."

"We would?" Angel asked, trying to fathom where Cordelia might be heading.

"Sure. That's so unglamorous. We need something . . . *cooler*."

Doyle nodded, showing excitement of his own. "Right. A vampire sports agent, now there's a winner. Going into negotiations, fangs bared, waiting for first blood. Show me the money—or I'll show you your spleen." He wilted beneath the glares Angel and Cordelia gave him. "It was just a thought."

"We need something cool," Cordelia said. "A vampire rock star? Top of the charts? Big production numbers? What do you think?"

Angel tried to think of anything to say that Cordelia wouldn't interpret as too negative. She could be overly protective of her ideas. "What would a vampire rock star do?"

"I don't know," Cordelia admitted. "I haven't gotten that far with the concept yet. But we could probably get a killer soundtrack deal from it, too. Have really cool weekly guest stars." She looked at Angel. "Can you sing?"

"No," Angel said quickly, trying not to think about Cordelia's concept too deeply.

"A vampire rock star's too passé," Doyle commented. "The detective thing could work. It would just have to be handled a bit differently. Upscaled. Sort of a *Charlie's Angels* meets *Salem's Lot* take."

Cordelia's brow furrowed. "The vampire kind of behind the scenes?"

Doyle nodded. "Letting his beautiful associates handle the cases."

"Beautiful associates?" Cordelia mused. "Maybe we could have just one. Who's really good at her job. Very sexy. Very cute."

"And a charming, debonair male associate," Doyle agreed. "Just to kind of keep things balanced. Keep both sides of the demographics happy, you know."

"You?"

Doyle looked insecure. "There's something wrong with me?"

"You don't even know all the romance languages."

Doyle sighed. "Russian is not a romance language."

Three young men entered the bar from the street outside. They moved easily, with an innate grace that Angel noticed at once. The fluid movement was only one of the indications the three vampires weren't new to unlife.

While Doyle and Cordelia continued to plot, Angel watched the three vampires as they quietly took a table in the corner. They watched the bar's clientele with predators' hooded, hungry eyes.

A few minutes passed, and a young couple got up from a booth and headed for the door at the back of the bar. The three vampires got up together without exchanging a word. They flowed through the bar in pursuit of their prey.

"Hey, Wally," Doyle called out during a commercial break in *Dark Midnight*. "Maybe you can settle a small bet."

"The Kings tanked the game," the bartender replied. "Yuan called over, said he thought you might be here. He wants you to pay up."

Doyle waved it away. "The Lakers are still playing. I've got a good feeling. Anyway, do you know if Russian is one of the five romance languages?"

"Depends, mate," Wally said. "If she's listening and not screaming at you, I'd say that's romantic."

"It's Romanian," Angel said as he got to his feet. "That's the fifth language. I'll be back."

"Was that them?" Doyle asked.

"Yes."

"Would you like some help?"

"No." Angel paused, thinking the answer might have been a little sudden. "Really. Enjoy the show, the time away from work. If I couldn't handle this on my own, I'd be the first to say so."

They looked at him in silence, making him feel a little more uncomfortable.

Angel felt awkward. The whole let's-be-friends-and-do-good-as-investigators thing got a little close at times. Only Buffy had been closer, and maybe he hadn't handled that as well as he could have. Of course, they hadn't counted on the vampire-makes-love-to-love-of-life-and-goes-insane event.

Angel pointed at the back door, aware that precious seconds were ticking away. "Lives to save."

Cordelia nodded, but she still didn't look happy about the whole situation. "Go on. We don't want to hold you up. Clock's ticking."

"The hero thing," Doyle said. "We understand."

"But if you need help," Cordelia said, "just whistle."

"Whistle. Got it." Angel followed his pointing finger through the back doors and into the alley. The three vampires had used their time well, quickly surrounding the couple and cutting off escape routes.

The young couple looked as if they were slumming. Both were dressed in leather, *GQ* and Victoria's Secret respectively, looking to get a buzz from traipsing through the dangerous underbelly of the city and take it to the condo.

"Stay back!" the young brunette screamed as she dug frantically in her purse and came out with Mace. She held the tube threateningly.

The vampires only laughed, genuinely amused. They dressed like skaters, buzz-cut hair stained neon colors—blue, orange, and green—and sported facial piercings.

The woman's husband or boyfriend struck a martial arts pose. He had the form right, but the movements were too stiff. He yelled, "Ki-yah!"

The lead vampire stepped in suddenly, feinted,

then kicked the man's legs from under him, spilling him into the alley.

"Lance!" the young woman screamed.

"Stay back, Becca!" The young man tried to get to his feet.

The lead vampire kicked his hands out from under him.

Becca lunged forward, spraying the lead vampire full in the face. The Mace deluge was so thick it left droplets.

"Not exactly Teen Spirit," the vampire stated calmly. He morphed, revealing the monster that had claimed his soul, and bared his fangs. He licked the Mace from his upper lip. "Kind of tame."

Becca screamed, followed almost immediately by Lance as they realized the horror they faced was much worse than they'd believed. Becca grabbed Lance's shoulder and almost jerked him to his feet. They retreated back into the rear of the building on the other side of the alley, and there was suddenly nowhere else to go. They screamed.

The three vampires closed in.

"Hey, guys," Angel spoke softly.

In less than a heartbeat all three vampires faced him.

"Private party?" Angel showed them his empty hands. "Or can anybody play?"

The vampire leader jerked his head at the green-haired vampire. "Take him, Boz."

Without a word, Boz hurled himself at Angel, drawing a sword from under his long coat.

Moving with blinding speed, Angel flexed his wrist, shooting out the spring-loaded stake he'd hidden up his sleeve. The wooden stake thudded into the vampire's chest with a meaty smack, carrying enough force to rock him back on his heels.

Disbelief stained the vampire's features, then he exploded into dust.

Angel fell into a ready stance facing the remaining two vampires, who realized there was something different about their challenger. "I never come empty-handed," Angel said. "I brought a party favor." He pointed his other hand at the lead vampire and twisted his wrist. The stake leaped forward.

The vampire leader grabbed a trashcan lid and blocked the stake, letting it embed in the galvanized metal with a loud *whang!* He spun, folding the trash can lid down like a Frisbee, and flinging it.

Angel dodged and the spinning trash can lid missed him by less than an inch. It hit the alley wall and dug deeply into the concrete and mortar, quivering as over a third of it buried into the wall.

The other vampire unwrapped a fine-linked

Japanese-style chain and grappling hook from his waist. The chain was nearly ten feet long and the grappling hook was as big as Angel's hand. The vampire whirled the hook around his head while the leader drew a pair of sais from his shirtsleeves. They looked like daggers, but instead of blades, they had long center spikes flanked by two other spikes.

"Got some party favors of our own," the vampire leader said, twirling the sais.

The vampire whirling the grappling hook let fly at Angel's head.

A woman's bloodcurdling scream echoed inside the bar. A few of the tavern's patrons finished their drinks and headed out, but the rest of them pulled in closer together and ignored the scream.

"Maybe I should go check on things," Doyle suggested.

"No," Cordelia replied. "If Angel wanted us there, he'd tell us." She cupped one ear. "No whistle."

A loud smash sounded through the back door, followed by the roar of animals.

Doyle felt guilty about not going into the alley, but Cordelia was right. There'd been no whistle. *Of course, it's kind of hard to whistle when a vampire's ripping your head off.*

"You're probably right," he said. After all, Angel

was the warrior among them. Doyle only fought when he couldn't talk or buy his way out of trouble. And that was only trouble he couldn't duck or outrun.

"We'd be in his way," Cordelia said. "Three vampires. Small alley. They don't stand a chance."

Something thumped loudly against the back door, warping it in the frame.

"At least," Cordelia went on, "not much of a chance. Maybe."

Doyle peeled the label from his empty bottle and tried not to think about the fight in the alley. Angel would call if he needed help.

The television drew Doyle's attention again. He studied Whitney Tyler and wished there were a way to check on the Lakers score. "You know, there may be something more here than meets the eye."

Cordelia wrote brief notes on the *Variety* trade magazine. "Like what?"

"Well"—Doyle shifted in the booth—"granted that Angel wasn't exactly in what one would call an ebullient mood, he seemed to turn even more dour after he'd seen the lady up there."

"He said she reminded him of someone."

"You gotta wonder who she was, her leaving an impression like that, I mean." Doyle ignored the metallic clatter that rang along the bar's back wall.

Shrugging, Cordelia said, "A vampire hors d'oeuvre."

Doyle studied the actress as she scaled a building, trying to see in her what Angel had seen. *Maybe Angel sees something else in her, but all I see is one fine-looking woman.* He checked his watch, knowing the Lakers game should be close to finishing.

Cordelia's note-taking finally got the better of his curiosity, and pursuing that was a lot better than thinking about what was going on in the alley. "What are you doing there?" he asked.

"Making notes."

Doyle nodded. "You see, I kinda had that figured. I was wondering what those notes were about."

"The television show."

Grinning, Doyle said, "You wouldn't have to take notes if you just popped a blank videocassette in the VCR. That way you could watch it over again if you wanted."

Cordelia rolled her eyes. "Not this show. If I wanted to keep up with *Dark Midnight,* I'd just get a few copies of *TV Guide* or jump on a Web site."

"Then what show?"

"The one I'm going to pitch. The *Charlie's Angels* with vampire."

"Oh." Doyle didn't have anything to say to that. Since he'd gotten to meet Cordelia Chase, he'd had to admit she was the most fascinating creature he'd met since—well, in a long, long time. "You're really going to pursue this?"

"Duh," Cordelia said sarcastically. "Do you know how much money you can make from a series idea that goes into syndication?"

"No."

Cordelia considered that. "Okay, neither do I, but that doesn't matter. Whatever it is, it's a lot. Enough to get me out of that crummy—" She paused. "Enough to get me into an apartment I deserve. Maybe enough left over to get a good car. A few other things."

Something that groaned in pain bounced from the bar's back doors. Roars rumbled from outside, growing in intensity.

Wally the bartender picked up the phone and pulled a shotgun from under the bar. Evidently he'd become convinced the action outside was going to spill back into the bar.

The migraine seized Doyle without warning, feeling as if it was going to split his head in two. He lost motor control and dropped forward heavily, his forehead thudding against the tabletop. He hadn't become aware of his demon heritage till only a few years ago.

Dealing with the fact that he could willingly change from human form to something a lot stronger and faster, something with blue-green skin and a spiky face, had been hard enough. But the Powers That Be went on to grant him—or curse him—with the ability to have visions of people in trouble. After that, he'd been given the directive to find Angel in L.A. and team up with him. Despite the dangerous work and sometimes thankless task, Doyle had gotten to enjoy the cases Angel Investigations took on.

But the vision reception had never gotten any more fun.

Sight of the bar's interior went away, replaced by what looked like a television set. Whitney sat in the radio booth set from the series taking calls. This time it was very clear the radio station was a television set complete with camera and sound crews. Then the image changed again, shifting to an ocean scene at night. A young woman with a sword who looked just like Whitney Tyler stood on a pitching, rain-soaked ship's deck. Her clothing looked as if it came from a movie set nearly three hundred years ago.

Why would I see something like that? Doyle wondered. He surfaced from the vision for just an instant, the pain subsiding but not quite going away.

A word formed in the back of his mind so strongly he had no choice but to speak it. *"Atonement."*

"What?"

Doyle lifted his head carefully, hammered by the residual pain left over by the vision. Drool ran down to his chin, cold in the tavern's air-conditioning. He glanced over at Wally, who was talking rapidly on the phone while brandishing the shotgun.

"Did I say something?" Doyle asked.

"It sounded like 'a ton of mint,' " Cordelia said.

"Atonement," Doyle corrected.

"Whatever."

"Why would I say that?"

"It was your vision."

"Right. I need to speak to Angel." Doyle put a palm firmly against his forehead between his eyes and rubbed. Sirens sounded in the distance, but he knew they'd get closer. Maybe Angel hadn't needed their help earlier, but he was betting they wouldn't be turned down with the police closing in. "And I'd say we've about worn out our welcome here." He patted his pockets, but came up empty. He looked at Cordelia, totally embarrassed. "I don't think Angel quite settled up our tab yet."

"You're going to pay me back," Cordelia insisted as she rummaged in her purse and brought out a few bills.

Doyle nodded earnestly. "Of course. I wouldn't dream of welching on a debt."

Cordelia put the money on the table. "After all, I know where you work."

"Hey," Wally called from the bar, the phone held tight to one ear while he held the shotgun in the other, "wasn't that your mate that just went out into the alley, Doyle? You gonna leave him in that world of hurt?"

"If it was my friend," Doyle replied, "he'd whistle."

"Whistle?"

"He'd scream out for help," Cordelia said. She pinched the inside of Doyle's arm fiercely.

"Ow!" Doyle pulled his arm away.

"Don't give away all our secret modus operandi," Cordelia whispered. "You tell Wally about the whistle signal, Wally tells somebody else about the whistle signal, soon everybody knows and then what's the use of having a signal?"

Doyle rubbed the painful area on the inside of his arm. "Right. Got it. Maybe you could get my attention some other way next time."

"I didn't have a two-by-four handy."

Doyle took Cordelia by the arm and headed for the back door. He wasn't sure what the vision meant yet, but there was no doubt that he needed to tell Angel.

❖　　❖　　❖

Angel spun away from the sai that flashed for his head, moving back into the strike set up by the man with the grappling hook and chain. The two vampires had obviously fought together for a long time. Their experience reflected in the way they moved together, with hardly a word spoken between them.

The couple Angel had come to rescue stood frozen against the other side of the alley. At first he'd thought they were too terrified to move, then he'd noticed the rapt looks on their faces. At this point they were willing observers, evidently thinking their little slumming party was turning up more excitement than they'd anticipated. Unfortunately, they were also in the way.

The grappling hook whipped through the air for Angel's feet. He stabbed his arms out and leaped, turning a flip in the air and landing on his feet again. The vampire with the sais was already moving on him as the grappling hook struck sparks from the concrete wall behind where he'd stood.

The approaching police sirens pierced the air and echoed in the alley, trapped between the buildings.

Angel grabbed a shipping pallet from the ground and used it for defense. The sai snapped through the cheap pine ribs, nearly cutting the pallet in half with a series of firecracker pops.

Dropping to the ground as the swordsman cut the air over his head, Angel lashed out with a foot, kicking his opponent's feet out from under him. The vampire came up and went down, caught by surprise and taken off balance. He landed on his back and tried to recover.

Angel lunged, ripping one of the broken boards from the shipping pallet. Still on his back, partially stunned and having no time to recover, the vampire swung his weapon at Angel. Straightening his arm, Angel blocked the sai stroke, then slammed the broken wood through the vampire's heart.

The vampire tried another sai blow but turned to dust before it could be completed. The sai clanged when it dropped and struck the ground.

The chain rattled and hissed as it sliced through the air.

Angel threw himself to the side and grabbed the first vampire's fallen sword. He rolled and narrowly avoided the grappling hook. The sharp prong knocked chips from the pavement.

"You're going to die now," the third vampire promised. "You killed Johann and Boz, but you aren't going to take me." His face was a mask of vampiric ferocity and hate. The slitted eyes glittered. He popped the grappling hook and chain back, then whirled it around his head again.

Angel pushed himself to his feet. "I'm two for two," he reminded in a soft, threatening voice.

"You're one of us." The vampire started circling, using all the available space in the alley. "Why defend them?"

Keeping the sword in front of him, set to block, Angel said, "If you have to ask, you wouldn't understand."

The sirens sounded even closer, and the strobing blue and red lights flashed in the street outside the alley. At that instant Cordelia and Doyle stepped through the tavern door, obviously looking for him.

"Time to die," the vampire stated, letting the grappling hook fly.

Moonlight glinted on the linked steel as it streaked for Angel's chest. It had been thrown with enough force to punch through even vampire flesh and bone.

Distracted by the arrival of Cordelia and Doyle, Angel reacted almost too slowly. He slapped the sword into the chain and caused the grappling hook and a section of the chain to wrap around the blade. He grabbed the trapped chain with his free hand, set himself, and yanked.

The vampire flew through the air.

"Bad time?" Doyle asked.

"Get back to the office," Angel instructed. "I've only got one more to go. I'll talk to you there. And get those two out of here." He nodded at the couple.

Doyle nodded, took Cordelia by the arm, and hurried off. They pushed the couple ahead of them.

Angel tried to slip the sword free of the chain and grappling hook but couldn't because the decorative hilt was trapped in the links. He launched a spinning wheel kick. His heel connected with the vampire's face just as the first police car rolled into the alley.

The vampire rolled in the air and landed on his back. He sprang to his feet and bolted for the opposite end of the alley.

Angel followed immediately, throwing himself into the hunt. It was the closest he'd allowed himself to get caught by the police in a long time, but nailing his quarry was important. The three vampires had been responsible for nearly a dozen deaths in the area that he knew of. He grabbed the remaining length of chain as he pursued the vampire.

A chain-link fence divided the alley, standing ten feet tall and topped with strands of barbed wire. The vampire leaped up onto the fence and hooked his hands into it. He pushed hard, scampering up the fence and pulling himself up to the window ledge on the second floor. Bullets flared from the side of the building.

Angel hit the fence next, intending to pull himself up.

"Stay down!" one of the policemen from the car behind him yelled.

Staying wasn't an option. Angel knew if the vampire got away, the killing spree would continue. He gathered himself, tightening his grip on the sword in his fist. It was now or never.

He moved.

CHAPTER FOUR

Galway Bay, Ireland, 1758

Angelus dodged back, narrowly avoiding the young swordswoman's metal-sheathed wooden blade as she advanced across *Handsome Jack*'s stern deck. He smiled with bloodlust as he backed against the railing, his footing uncertain on the pitching deck.

The swordswoman pulled her weapon back quickly, circling to the right around the steering wheel. "Come, foul demonspawn, or have you no stomach for honest swordplay?" She taunted as confidently as she moved. And the metal-sheathed wooden weapon told Angel she knew the true nature of those she faced.

"In your impudence you knock on death's door, girl," Angelus threatened as he slid the cutlass free of the waist sash. Lightning flashed across the dark sky again, igniting pale fire from the wickedly curved blade.

She stepped rapidly forward, engaging him. Steel whipped before Angelus's eyes. If he hadn't been faster and stronger as a vampire, she might have taken him easily. The clangor of steel rasping on steel filled the air around him, muting the *whip-crack* of the sailcloth above and the smack of the waves against the pitching ship. Darla and Darius fought on the deck below with the rest of the vampire crew.

Grappled to *Lugh's Fancy*, *Handsome Jack* jerked and jumped like a fish hitting the end of a line. Had *Fancy* not been bigger and heavier from the cargo she carried, the sudden stops as *Handsome Jack* hit the ends of her tethers might not have been as pronounced. The fallen sails continued to billow as the prevailing winds clawed at them.

"You're human, girl," Angelus taunted. "Your flesh is weak. Despite your skill, you will tire. I will have you soon enough."

Exploding into action, the woman lunged forward.

Angelus let her have his left shoulder. As a vampire the wound wouldn't even be noticeable by tomorrow. He readied his own blade, intending to cut her cheek and rob her of a portion of the irritating confidence she showed by marring her beauty.

But when her blade entered his flesh, it burned like a hot poker, telling him the steel had either been blessed or had been dipped in holy water.

Angelus screamed in rage as the pain threw his own sword stroke off. He stumbled, instinctively drawing back from the blade. The wound in his arm smoked as if he'd been exposed to direct sunlight.

The woman pressed her attack, her blade dancing before her.

Even with all his speed and skill, Angelus barely preserved his own existence time and time again, stopping the blade just short. He beat back her attack with sheer strength and the iron-willed dark fury that filled him.

One of Darius's vampires came up quietly behind her, hand ax upraised. Angel grinned, knowing he was about to get the chance to exact his revenge for the pain.

Then the woman disengaged and spun without warning, dropping into a crouch, one leg bent under her and the other straight out. The hand ax split the air over her head. She took a two-handed grip on her sword and slashed the vampire across the midsection.

The vampire cursed as he backpedaled and tried to hold himself together. Before he could get away, the woman rose and drove her metal-encased wooden blade through his heart. He turned to dust and blew away.

Angelus struck from behind, trying to slash the woman across the backs of her knees and cripple her. Somehow, though, she sensed his attack and leaped high into the air. She pulled her knees in to her chest and flipped backward, coming down on her feet easily.

Angelus squared off with her again. He hungered to break her, to shatter her poise and confidence, to fill her with fear that would lace her blood with adrenaline, and then to drink deeply of her. He'd had—and enjoyed—numerous victims since Darla had sired him, but this was going to be a victory to be savored.

Even as Angelus prepared to strike, wood crunched and *Handsome Jack* rocked violently to the right. The deck slanted too steeply to stand on the rain-slicked wood, and Angelus fell toward the ocean. For a moment he thought the ship was going to roll over the rocky shoals it had gotten caught on.

He slid across the deck, flailing desperately. Before he reached the other side of the deck, already aiming for the railing and hoping it wouldn't tear loose, *Handsome Jack* righted, slapping back down into the bay. A wave washed over the side, sluicing the deck.

The woman had fallen from her feet as well, but she'd caught the stern railing with one hand. When the ship righted, she rolled to her feet, the blade before her.

Angelus pushed up as the woman rushed at him, barely blocking her blade from his throat. Mired on the rocky shoals, *Handsome Jack* bucked and reared like a wild horse under an unwanted rider.

The young woman didn't appear affected by the tumult. No matter where Angelus turned, no matter what defense he chose, her blade constantly battered at him. Retreating angrily, following the ship's railing, Angelus made his way to the front of the stern. He parried a lunge she made that would have skewered his liver if she'd connected. She continued to move, striking as fast as the lightning that ripped across the dark sky.

Cunningly, Angelus reached up for the billowing folds of the fallen sails. He yanked one down, tearing it free of the restraining lines as he dodged a thrust aimed at his neck. The heavy canvas fell, draping the young woman before she could move. He slashed at the canvas, aiming where he thought her head might be.

The keen blade ripped through the sailcloth

where she struggled to free herself. But even as the cutlass passed easily through the folds, Angelus knew he'd missed her. His foot twisted on the rain-slick deck, pulling him out of position with the force he'd used.

By the time he turned back around, swearing foully, the young woman's blade slit the canvas, carving a large opening. The heavy sailcloth dropped around her, collapsing to pool at her ankles. Her red-gold hair was rain-matted, strands hanging down into her face, masking the gray-green eyes that smoldered with hate.

"Moira!"

The desperate call cut through the waves crashing against *Handsome Jack*, the cries of wounded and dying amidships, and the ferocious roars of some of Darius's crew who'd gone feral. The young woman's head turned, and she sprinted for the stern railing. She didn't break stride, leaping onto the railing, then down.

Amazed at the decisive way she'd moved, Angelus walked to the railing and peered down.

The vampires had wreaked havoc on *Handsome Jack*'s crew and passengers. Corpses lay strewn over the amidships, given grotesque semilife by the waves that crashed over the sides and ran across the deck. The rushing water moved the dead limbs, sometimes strong enough to move a body a few feet as well. The jagged spar of the broken mast thrust up defiantly.

Moira, the swordswoman, landed on the deck in a crouch, one hand out to help keep her balance. A vampire turned toward her, and lightning flashed, showing the dark blood that stained his face. Moira's sword stabbed upward as she got to her feet. The blade slashed through the vampire's neck, decapitating him, and he died in a swirl of dust.

Already in motion, Moira rushed through the dusty remnants, aiming for the small group gathered at the forecastle railing. Pools of flaming oil, obviously from lanterns used as weapons against the vampires, guttered and slid greasily across the water sliding across the deck.

Darla stood near the hold, her nails deep in a man's flesh as she drank the life from him. Her party dress was tattered and bloodstained, no longer the beautiful confection she'd taken from a victim who'd bought it in Paris.

Darius headed up the other vampires, keeping the attacks up on the remaining victims. Four warriors among the humans kept the blood-maddened vampires at bay.

Angelus couldn't tell how many of Darius's crew had been slain in the battle because vampires didn't leave corpses behind other than those of people they'd killed. But Angelus knew that the vampire numbers had been whittled down considerably.

The warriors defended two older men in monk's habits as well as five elegantly clad men and women. Soaked as they were from the rain, the wealthy passengers no longer looked regal, only fearful as they pressed against the wall behind them.

Moira was among the vampires before Darius knew she was there. Her blade flicked out, slicing a vampire's head off. The head and body turned to dust before the head fell to the deck.

Using her action as a catalyst as the vampires suddenly realized there was a new danger among them, the four warriors pressed their attack. One swung a lantern at the nearest vampire, shattering the glass and spreading oil across him.

The wick clung to the vampire, the flame fluttering weakly for a moment in the wind and rain before rushing across the vampire. Whale oil burned brightly but had low heat. Still, the blue and yellow flames wreathed the vampire more quickly than he could put them out. He staggered away, howling in pain and fear as the fire ignited vampire flesh and burned him to ash.

The four warriors fought desperately, like a team that had been together for years. They spread their line but kept the protection over their charges. But the vampire numbers were still too much. A vampire raked sharp nails across one man's throat even as his blade severed the neck of his opponent. The warrior dropped to his knees, clutching at his ruined throat as crimson life deserted him, staring at the whirlwind of dust the vampire had become. Lightning flashed, revealing the dying man's glassy-eyed stare.

Angelus vaulted over the stern railing and landed on the deck below.

Darla turned to him, still feeding. Her eyes peered at him from her bloody visage. "Angelus," she called, smiling, blood dripping from her fangs, "have you found a new pretty to play with?"

Angelus grinned cockily. "I claim the woman as my own."

Darla laughed at him, discarding the corpse of the sailor whose life she'd drained. "Perhaps I should be jealous."

"You'd be jealous of a dead woman." He crossed the deck in long strides, closing on the final fight taking place. He ripped the shirtsleeve from his wounded arm. The jagged cut held red infection and swelling that made the flesh gape open. "She cut me, Darla. I didn't know I could be wounded like this anymore."

"When we return to town, we'll have to have that tended."

"I'll drink her blood!" Angelus roared. "That will be all the healing I need."

"These people are different, Angelus," Darla said in a more serious tone. "You've not seen anyone like them. They're fanatics, driven to follow their cause."

"So are the British, the Scots, and even the Irish," Angelus said.

"They are only men."

"And these are not?" Angelus watched as another vampire was struck down. Darius roared with rage, narrowly avoiding a pitch-and-tar torch one of the warriors wielded.

"They bleed and they die," Darla said, "but they are more than mere human. Their cause binds them and lifts them above that. You can kill them, but you must be careful."

Darla's words, delivered with more seriousness and cautiousness than he could remember, only made Angelus angrier. Since he'd been reborn, ripped from the grave by the evil that made him eternal with the night, he knew he was better than anyone and anything.

One of the warriors started praying in a loud voice. Exertion and fatigue, maybe even fear, made his words ragged. The sailcloth snapping overhead and the waves crashing booming thunder against *Handsome Jack*'s hull made the prayer even harder to hear. But the effect was notice-able.

The three surviving warriors and the swords-woman rallied, beating Darius and his vampire crew back. Glancing to his right, Angelus saw the longboat that was obviously their goal. Before their casualties had run so high, there had been too many to hope to make their escape in the boat.

Led by Moira, the warriors broke through the vampires' line.

Angelus reached the longboat first, evil firing his still heart. There was nothing more satisfying than stealing a person's last hope. He sheathed his cut-lass just as *Handsome Jack* slewed again, grating against the rocky shoals. The bottom tore out of the ship and Angelus felt it settle more heavily into the water. Peering over the side, he saw the dark ocean roiling around the hull, less than a foot below the deck. The ship was going down quickly.

The longboat held a small anchor in its bow that was used to moor it in shallow water. It had been casually forged, an arm-thick shaft of iron maybe a yard long. Angelus seized the anchor in both hands, lifted it, then drove it as hard as he could toward the longboat's bottom.

Lightning flickered through the sky, sketching long-fingered demon's claws, then thunder pealed, drowning out the sound of the longboat's bottom shattering. The anchor smashed through the wood, tearing out a huge hole a foot wide. The anchor thumped against the ship's deck, driving free long splinters there as well.

"No!" The swordswoman's cry echoed with hopeless dismay. She drew up only a few feet away, the other warriors, the monks, and the wealthy hot on her heels.

Relishing the terror he heard in her voice, Angelus drew his sword triumphantly, falling into a defensive position. "Yes!"

"You have killed us." Moira's gray-green eyes flashed angrily.

"Not yet," Angelus taunted. "But it won't be long now."

Without another word the swordswoman attacked, her blade streaking for Angelus's head. He parried her attack, feeling the ferocity and determination in her blade as it met his. He'd thought seeing the longboat destroyed would have taken the fight from her. The people they were protecting dropped to their knees and began wailing in fear. It was music to Angelus's ears.

The warriors' prayer echoed over *Handsome Jack* as the ship wallowed and sank even more. Waves cascaded across the deck, rolling from side to side as the ship rocked heavily. Few oil lanterns remained lit in the rigging, as if the light itself retreated from the darkness waiting to consume the last of *Handsome Jack*'s travelers.

"You can never win," Moira said, driving her sword at him.

Angelus blocked her blows, rarely having an opportunity to launch an attack of his own. He told himself it didn't matter, that time was on his side because *Handsome Jack* was going down, listing even worse. The rocky shoals grating the ship's hull sent vibrations along the deck.

Another warrior fell beneath the blade of one of Darius's crew, leaving the monks and the wealthy passengers open to more direct attack. The vampires seized them with impunity.

Then a harsh crack filled the air. *Handsome Jack* staggered. The uneven motion threw Angelus off-balance. The swordswoman's blade drew a thin line of fire along his right jaw. He cursed and tried to recover, gone from skill to primitive instinct as the deck jumped beneath him.

The woman swung again, and Angelus stepped inside the blow. Her arm crashed against his side, and her sword hilt hammered against his back. But the blade didn't touch him.

Angelus stood chest to chest with her, her body pressed almost intimately against his. His senses reeled as he scented the hot blood that coursed through her. Shadows warred with lantern light and lightning flashes to illuminate the high planes of her face. Her pulse beat in the dark hollow of her throat.

She tried to yank away, but Angelus trapped her arm, grabbing her above her elbow. There wasn't enough room for her to get the sword into play. Fire smoldered in her gray-green eyes as she stared into his.

"Never," she whispered, "will you take me."

Angelus felt the desire flare inside him. There was nothing human about it. If it was unleashed, he knew it would come dangerously close to consuming them both. He gazed at her neck where the hollow held her beating pulse, then bared his fangs.

Before he could touch her, her free hand came up with a cross. She pressed it against his mouth, searing his lips with a pain he had never known. Angelus pulled his head back, howling. Instinctively he grabbed her wrist and pulled the cross from his flesh. Her arm broke in his frenzied grip with a loud pop. Still, she struggled to get free.

Half-mad with the incredible agony, Angelus tightened his grip on her other arm and pulled it from the shoulder socket. She cried out, but he didn't care. The hunger took a backseat to the rage he felt. He slapped her, knocking her from him.

The young woman stumbled back, splashing through the inches-deep water that rolled across

Handsome Jack's deck. She tried to catch herself, but the broken arm and the dislocated one wouldn't hold her. She fell heavily.

Angelus reached a hand to his burned mouth, cursing. Bumpy blisters stood out under his fingertips, some of them already broken and running. He lurched after the woman, tightening his grip on his sword.

Handsome Jack reeled drunkenly again. Unable to keep his feet, Angelus collapsed to his knees. The waves raced across him, kissed silver by the moon and washing up over his waist now, drenching him. He stared at the swordswoman as she kicked herself backward to get away from him, her injured arms flopping uselessly at her sides.

Angelus tried to get up in the sudden deluge but couldn't quite make it. He wanted to kill the woman more than anything he'd wanted to do in his life or unlife.

The incoming waves fought with one another, creating a swirling pool in the center of the ship. Water sloshed up from the open cargo hold now, letting Angelus know the ship was filling fast.

Handsome Jack jerked again. The stern took a harsh dip into the ocean, water rushing over the railing.

Darla helped Angelus to his feet. "Let's go," she said.

"Wait," Angelus ordered through his mutilated lips, surging away from Darla angrily.

"There's no time."

Angelus wanted to protest, but he knew it was true. The ship was going down more quickly. He retreated, swearing at the woman.

Darius's crew was halved in number. The night's foray and strike against the moneyed nobility arriving in Galway hadn't gone as easily as Darius had predicted. Darius yelled his crew into motion. Three vampires grabbed hand axes and cut free the ropes tying them to the floundering ship. *Fancy* heeled over hard to its side, pulled dangerously close to the storm-tossed sea.

"Cut her loose!" Darius roared as he took *Fancy*'s helm. "Get that damned ship cut loose quick, or she's gonna drag us down with her!"

The axes fell awkwardly, but the lines were slashed with basso *sproings* caused by the wet hawser ropes.

Angelus felt numb as he watched the broken-armed figure on board *Handsome Jack* struggling weakly to get to her feet. He still hungered for her, wanted to finish what he'd started.

Lightning carved the heavens, and thunder cannonaded around them as the final grappling lines were cut. *Handsome Jack* rolled over, sinking quickly beneath the waves. Darius got *Fancy* under way after a fierce struggle to get the sails back into play and escape the undertow created by *Handsome Jack*'s sinking.

Angelus watched as the sea drank the ship down. Even over the rolling thunder he was somehow able to hear a woman's chanting voice. Even through the darkened distance, he knew her eyes were on him, hating him with everything she had left. He smiled at that thought, knowing she was taking it with her to the grave.

Then *Handsome Jack* gave a final lurch, rolled over, and passed beneath the waves.

CHAPTER FIVE

"Whitney Tyler: Where did she come from and how did she get the lead in today's hottest show on television?" Cordelia asked.

Doyle glanced at Cordelia as he opened the door to the main office at Angel Investigations. "Well, I've got to admit, you've got me there." He checked the hallway out of habit.

Even in the short time they'd been there, he'd learned there was no telling who'd show up at Angel's door. As surely as Angel was driven to help those who needed help, those who needed help were driven to seek him out. It tended to be one big, vicious circle, and sometimes the lines blurred.

The hallway was, thankfully, empty.

Cordelia peered intently into the plate-glass window to the left of the door where closed venetian blinds prevented a view into the office.

Doyle put a foot against the door, bracing it so it wouldn't open without going through his foot. *Of course, that is possible.* He peered into the window as well. He couldn't see through the Venetian blinds. He lowered his voice to a whisper. "Do you see something?"

Cordelia looked at him perplexedly and lowered her voice as well. "Why are you whispering?"

"Well, if you saw something in the office," Doyle explained, still whispering, "I didn't want to warn it. Or him. Or her. Or them." *Get a grip, Doyle.* One of the awkward byproducts of having a vision was suffering from a hyperactive imagination for a few hours afterward.

"You saw something in the office?" Cordelia took a step back.

"No," Doyle explained patiently, "I thought you saw something in the window."

"I did." Cordelia touched her hair. "I got my hair cut and styled yesterday."

Doyle nodded. "I thought I noticed it looked a little—" He hesitated, waiting for the lead he needed.

"Short." Cordelia grimaced and patted her hair into place. "You noticed it, too."

Actually, Doyle hadn't noticed. *There's gotta be a book somewhere,* he lamented. *When to notice, when not to notice, what to notice, how to properly say what you did or did not notice about a woman's hair.* But he nodded. "I thought that a little shorter looked—"

"Short." Cordelia's nostrils flared a little as she peered back into the window and did the fluff thing to her hair with her fingers.

"Ah," Doyle said, "fuming."

"What?"

Doyle put outraged steel in his voice. "I said, damnit, if you can't trust your stylist, who can you trust?" He opened the office door and went in.

"She knew I was trying out for the Tarantino thing." Cordy followed him inside.

Doyle flipped on the lights and chased the shadows that habitually formed in the office. Secondhand furniture held down the carpet, strategically covering the worst of the stains.

"Coffee?" Cordelia asked as she sat at the desk in front of the computer and brought it up.

"Sure." Doyle dropped into a nearby chair.

Cordelia pointed without looking. "The pot's over there."

Doyle looked at the machine. "Oh, yeah, right. What was I thinking?" He got up and started to punch the button.

"That's the third time for the first filter," Cordelia said. "Keep the grounds but get a fresh filter. Only use half the water to get the coffee up to strength."

Doyle searched the cabinet and made the substitution. Coffee was another thing the Angel Investigations team made stretch during the lean times. When the water was trickling through, he returned to his seat.

Quietly he watched Cordelia's assault on the computer. She'd gotten much better at accessing information over the Internet since she'd started working for Angel. But no matter what, he'd found he could stare at Cordelia Chase for hours and be happy about it. He just couldn't quite figure out a way to tell her that. Facing hellbeasts was easier than thinking about dealing with a rejection from Cordelia.

"What are you looking at?" Cordelia asked.

Looking at Cordelia is good, Doyle thought, *but getting caught looking totally blows.* "I didn't want to interrupt you."

"You're not."

"I was curious about the Whitney Tyler reference you made earlier."

"I was just thinking that researching how Whitney got on *Dark Midnight* might help me better pitch my own series proposal. And since you had the vision about her, I knew we'd have to research her."

Doyle nodded. "Sounds like a plan." Now that the coffee had been made, he got up and filled two cups. He placed Cordelia's cup beside her. "So how do you think she got the part?"

"Casting couch," Cordelia responded. "Definitely. Oh, the *Enquirer* and the *Star* may not have gotten the goods on exactly who and what yet, but they will."

"You feel very strongly about that, do you?"

"And how else do you think someone would get to the number-one-rated show this television season? Get real."

Doyle scratched the back of his neck. "Actually, I still kind of like the idea that everybody with talent gets a break when the time comes. Call me old-fashioned if you want."

"If that was true, I'd have my own series by now, too. What talented person is more deserving of a break—and a starring vehicle role, I might add—than me?" Cordelia gave him a bright, winning smile.

"I'm not going to argue that," Doyle said earnestly.

"So how do you think she got the role?"

Doyle shrugged, wondering how to give a straight answer that he knew Cordelia wasn't going to like. "Maybe the producers saw Whitney in something else, decided she'd make a great vampire radio shock jock."

"No way," Cordelia said. "Not for a number-one show."

"Maybe at first they didn't have the number-one-show angle figured."

"Please. How can you not figure a number-one show?"

Doyle sighed. "Right."

"And what kind of production do you think the show's sponsors would have seen her in to make them say, 'That girl, that's the girl we want.' Oh, please, that's so very fairy tale."

"I don't know," Doyle replied, feeling more than a little defensive. What was it about Cordelia that kept him hanging around like a moth drawn to a flame? He looked at her again, didn't get caught and therefore felt pretty good about his already improved surveillance techniques, and remembered what the attraction was. Well, part of it anyway. He'd still never met anyone who thought like Cordelia Chase. He shook his head. "Man, that just rips away a lot of fantasies."

"You're a big boy with a life that's kind of going nowhere fast. You'll create more fantasies."

"Ouch." Doyle peered over Cordelia's shoulder at the images of Whitney on the *Dark Midnight* set. "What have we got here?"

"One of the official Whitney fan club websites." Cordelia moved the cursor around the various thumbnails of pictures.

"Any information on Whitney pre-*Dark Midnight*?" Doyle stood up and moved behind her, peering in more closely. The visions he had were seldom self-explanatory.

"I'm going there now." The computer monitor image shivered, exploding into thousands of colorful pixels like a July Fourth fireworks display.

When the new images sprang up, Doyle felt cold cat's claws creeping up his spine, touching that inhuman side of himself he kept pressed back into a distant corner of his mind when he could.

One of the pictures on the new page showed Whitney dressed in breeches and a blouse and holding a sword. The half-demon's memory shorted into overload for a moment, overlaying the computer picture with the vision image he'd had at Wally's. This was obviously what he'd been shown.

"What's wrong?" Cordelia asked.

Doyle shrugged. "Well, she looks a lot like the young woman in my vision. But not exactly."

"Does it have to be exact?"

"No," Doyle replied. "You just kind of see what's there and have to figure out the rest. But this is close."

"Well, this is off-Broadway. Shakespeare. The guy who's made a comeback with a few movies lately." Cordelia scrolled through the information available. "Whitney's supposed to be twenty-seven years old. Well, you can bet that's off by five or ten years. With a good makeup guy in this business you can get away with murder."

"It looks like someone got away with murder."

Doyle pointed to the small inset picture in the lower left corner that caught his attention. A big banner read MURDERERS STILL AT LARGE. "Tobin Calhoun. Remember him?"

"Oh, yeah. His murder two years ago made all the Hollywood gossip columns and the major news shows. For about a month. They called it a tragedy, a true star about to be born, then everybody moved on to the next murder and scandal. The movie Calhoun was working on when he got killed just got released last summer. *Redline Heat*, the stock-car racing movie the producers thought would turn him into another Tom Cruise. That *so* wouldn't have happened. The movie totally tanked at the box office."

"As I remember," Doyle said, "Calhoun was kind of busy being dead at the time. He didn't make the usual pre-movie open barrage of Leno, Letterman, Oprah. I'd think it would be hard to draw an audience."

"We're talking Hollywood and the real world here," Cordelia objected. "If Calhoun had gotten to be a real big box-office draw, he'd have been missed more. Or longer, depending on how you want to judge that. By the fans, by the producers, etcetera. When it comes to fame, he made it bigger as a murder victim. There are probably still moviegoers out there who are wondering when Calhoun's going to come out with his next movie."

That's scary, Doyle realized, *and probably true.* "See if you can bring up the story. How was he tied in with Whitney Tyler?"

Cordelia tapped the keyboard. The inset picture exploded across the monitor and lines of text quickly scrolled onto the screen. "Says here she was dating him. It wasn't anything serious, though. Hmmmm. Maybe we want to check into that. Whitney had a small part in the movie. Calhoun's girlfriend or sister or something." She frowned. "That's really strange, but I don't remember much about her."

"Maybe she wasn't covered in the news very much."

"She must have had a terrible agent," Cordelia said. "You just can't buy that kind of publicity."

Doyle read for himself. He didn't have Cordelia's interest in the entertainment field, and his last two years before getting the assignment by the Powers That Be had been kind of self-involved.

According to the story, Calhoun had been waiting for Whitney Tyler down in the lobby of the apartment building where she lived. Gossip—at least on this particular website—had it that their on-screen romance had heated up to the real thing during the filming of the movie. At the time of the murder, the cast and crew were currently finishing

up the post-production shooting, working in bits
and pieces of scenes written in by the script doc-
tors hired to salvage the movie.

In broad daylight, with security in the building,
an assailant or assailants had abducted Calhoun,
taken him to a third-story glass-enclosed passage
to the building across one of the two streets the
apartment building faced, and beat him to death.
After nearly every bone in Calhoun's body had
been broken, the killer or killers had smashed the
glass out and hung the corpse out over the street.

No one had seen anything.

"Maybe we should find out a little more information about the murder," Doyle suggested.

"Halt!"

Ignoring the shouted command from the police
officer running from the far end of the alley, Angel
grabbed the fence bisecting the alley and scram-
bled up. Bullets struck sparks from the chain-links
and started a medley of ringing clanks. At the top
of the fence he avoided the barbed wire and
leaped to the second-story window ledge the vampire he pursued had gone through.

Angel dived into the room and rolled to his feet.
Glass crunched underfoot. He peered around the
empty bedroom, glad that no one was there. He'd
known it would be unoccupied because the vam-

pire he was chasing wouldn't have been able to enter if it had been someone's home.

The vampire hadn't hesitated at the front door. It hung in tatters in the doorframe, shards scattered before it out into the narrow hallway.

Angel coiled the grappling-hook chain around his arm as he passed through the doorway. A few of the doors along the passageway were open, and frightened faces peered out.

"Police," Angel said, pulling his coat aside to reveal his belt buckle like there was a badge there as well. The move had been choreographed by countless movies, and most people thought they saw the badge there. "I'm after the man that came through here."

A large man in a white T-shirt and Bettie Page Jungle Girl boxers pointed to the left, indicating the door at the end of the hallway.

"Thanks," Angel said. He ran, hoping to catch the fleeing vampire before he got away or the police managed to secure the area and make escaping almost impossible.

The door opened into a dimly lit stairwell.

Angel peered down, listening intently. He heard people's hoarse, fearful whispers, the whine of police sirens coming from out on the street, and the low-key hum of television programs. Somewhere above, someone was playing John Lee Hooker blues.

And the pounding of fleeing feet came from above, not below.

Angel ran up the stairs, ricocheting off the walls as he strove to go faster. He peered up the center of the stairwell and spotted the vampire peering back down at him two stair flights above.

"They're going to catch us both," the vampire said. "If we split up, we have a better chance."

Angel kept moving, not bothering to reply. Too many people had died because of the three vampires.

Cursing, another floor closer now, the vampire started running again.

At the sixth-floor landing, the stairwell ended facing a final row of apartments. When Angel stepped through the door, the vampire was nowhere in sight.

Moving more cautiously, aware that his prey could move almost soundlessly, Angel moved to the first door on the left. He didn't have to knock to feel the sanctuary of the home someone had made inside. If he couldn't pass the threshold, neither could the guy he was looking for.

He continued, starting to move more quickly because every room was occupied. It appeared more certain the vampire had already exited the floor through the rooftop access at the other end of the passageway.

Angel put his hand on the handle to the rooftop access door. The scuff of a foot across the carpet was slight, but it saved his life. He ducked and the vampire swung a fire ax into the door, shattering it with a loud crash.

Down the hallway, a door swung open. "What the hell is going on?" a man's voice demanded.

Angel rose, but the vampire was waiting. The ax handle caught Angel under the chin and knocked him onto his back several feet away. Slightly dazed, he watched as the vampire deliberated between trying to kill him or escaping.

Discretion was obviously the better choice of valor at the moment. The vampire turned and fled up the tight, spiral metal staircase leading to the rooftop.

Angel lunged to his feet and followed. He rounded the spiral staircase, and for a moment it felt as if he were back on *Handsome Jack*'s pitching deck in the stormy sea more than two hundred years ago. He remembered the predatory lust that had fired him as he'd pursued the young swordswoman.

Guilt hammered him, but he clung to it, using it to drive himself harder. He couldn't turn back the clock and save the swordswoman no matter how hard he tried. But once he put this vampire down, he'd be another step closer to the redemption he so desperately sought.

He pushed up at the rooftop access door and went through. Light hovered around the edges of the roof from the streetlights below. Footsteps crunched on the tar-and-gravel roof as sirens echoed up from below. Red and blue lights flashed against the nearby buildings. Frantic voices called out to one another.

Angel shook the chain loose from his arm as he ran, gathering the links up in loops like a cowboy with a lasso. He dropped the sword he still carried.

The vampire raced across the rooftop, weaving around the HVAC units that squatted there like fat, gray mechanical toads humming with the sound of worn bearings.

Taking the end of the chain with the grappling hook, Angel ran after the vampire, closing the distance with longer strides. He spun the grappling hook over his head, distracted by the sudden spotlight that descended over him a second before the sound of the helicopter's rotors reached his ears.

"This is the LAPD," a stern voice announced over an onboard PA system. "You are under arrest. Lie down on your stomach with your hands behind your head."

The vampire never slowed as he reached the rooftop's edge. He put one foot on the edge and leaped into the air, aiming for the building on the other side of the street.

Angel knew he could make the leap as well, but he couldn't let the chase go on that long. Already the police helicopter was close enough to buffet him with strong winds. He took a stake from his coat pocket and jammed it between the three bent rods that made up the grappling hook so that it stuck out. Then he threw the grappling hook as hard as he could, hoping for some kind of accuracy.

The grappling hook sped true, penetrating the vampire's back nearly six inches below his heart, which was the intended target.

Angel set himself with one foot on the roof's edge. The gleam of light on metal in front of the vampire told Angel the grappling hook had gone all the way through the vampire's body.

Setting himself, Angel leaned back and took up slack, holding the chain tightly. The vampire hit the end of the chain, coming to a sudden stop against the grappling hook less than ten feet from the building on the other side of the street. Gravity took over and the vampire fell.

Angel kept the chain taut, bracing himself as the vampire swung back against the apartment building.

"Repeat, this is the Los Angeles Police Department. Down on your face with your hands behind your head, or we will be forced to take action."

The vampire smashed into the side of the building three stories down with enough force to seriously injure anything human. But the vampire only snarled, reaching for the chain and starting to haul himself up the links.

Angel released the chain, sending the vampire plunging down nearly five feet. Then Angel tightened his grip on the chain again and pulled up as hard as he could.

At the end of the chain the grappling hook pulled up against the force of gravity that drew the vampire down. Between the slack and the sudden whip-crack motion Angel triggered, the grappling hook ripped through the vampire's flesh, cleaving the heart with the wooden stake jammed into it. With a final growl of rage and fear, the vampire turned into dust.

Angel hauled the chain up and glanced at the helicopter hovering above the rooftop. He slitted his eyes against the fierce intensity of the spotlight. He barely made out the man with the assault rifle clinging to the helicopter's side.

"Last chance, buddy," the PA blared. Bullets drilled the rooftop, sending gravel flying, but the spotlight lifted.

Angel ran in the opposite direction than the vampire had chosen. He leaped the distance between buildings and kept going across the rooftops.

Doyle flipped through the pages Cordelia had printed out for him concerning Tobin Calhoun's murder. He sighed and sipped the weak coffee, lamenting the taste as well as the watery complexion.

"Find anything?" Cordelia asked.

"No." Doyle dropped the papers on the floor and ran his fingers through his hair. He checked the time. "Angel's been gone awhile."

"He's okay." Cordelia continued tapping the keyboard.

"How do you know that?"

"Because you'd know if something happened to him."

Doyle remained quiet.

Cordelia stopped tapping the keyboard and looked at him. "You would, right?"

"I don't know."

"You were drawn to him, Doyle. That psychic thingy that brought you to him. That's some kind of bond. You'd know."

"Not really. The Powers That Be didn't exactly give me an owner's manual when they equipped me."

"You wouldn't know if something happened to Angel?"

Doyle shrugged, feeling guilty because it seemed as if he was letting Cordelia down in some way. Of course, it didn't help that she sounded really accusing. He decided he should be more confident. Even a woman like Cordelia should respond to confidence in a man. He squared his shoulders. "I'm really sure that I don't know if I would know if something happened to Angel. But I think I would."

Cordelia blinked.

"At least, you know"—Doyle turned a palm up—"it stands to reason I'd know." He paused. "Don't you think?" He stood. "Maybe we could go have a peek."

"He'd call." Cordelia turned her attention back to the monitor.

Doyle felt torn. On one hand he thought maybe they should go look for Angel, but on the other that definitely didn't sound safe.

Abruptly the desk phone rang.

Cordelia punched the speaker function automatically. She waited till the answering machine kicked in. "Angel?"

"Actually I was hoping to speak with someone at Angel Investigations." The man's voice sounded hesitant. "My name is Gunnar Schend. I'm the producer on *Dark Midnight*. It's a television show. Maybe I've got the wrong number."

"Wait," Cordelia pleaded as she punched the speaker phone function. "You've got the right number. This is Angel Investigations."

"It's not too late?" Schend asked.

"We never sleep," Cordelia assured him. "At least, the dark, brooding part of us never sleeps."

CHAPTER SIX

"There you are, man. I was starting to get seriously worried." Doyle appeared relieved.

Stepping up from the sewer tunnel entrance to his private rooms below the offices, Angel looked at Doyle, who stood on the stairs. "About the vampires?"

"Not that. Figured you could handle yourself there." Doyle shrugged. "At least, you said you could."

Angel closed the sewer hatch. "Is something wrong?"

Quickly Doyle summed up the vision he'd had, letting Angel know the present interest in Whitney Tyler was something the Powers That Be wanted him to look into as well as part of his own redemption.

At the end of Doyle's report Angel felt vaguely

uneasy. The memory of the swordswoman on *Handsome Jack* was more acute than most he had of those times. It had to mean something.

"And to top that off," Doyle said, "Gunnar Schend, Whitney Tyler's producer, is upstairs in the office with Cordelia."

Angel took the news in stride. The evening had started out in left field, so it was no surprise to see that things remained twisted and out of his control. "Is Schend alone?"

"You mean, is the woman with him?"

"Yeah, I guess I mean that."

"No. He's come alone."

"Let's go," Angel suggested, taking the lead up the stairs to the offices.

Gunnar Schend was twenty-something and wore dark sunglasses even though it was night. Dressed in Levi's, a white T-shirt, square-toed boots, and a black leather Harley-Davidson motorcycle jacket, he also wasn't quite the image of Hollywood that Angel expected. The dark tan was pure fake-bake. His hair was bleached the color of old ivory, moussed till it stood as at attention as a Buckingham Palace guard, carefully matching the French tickler on his chin.

The television producer moved restlessly, pacing back and forth in front of the desk. Cordelia sat on one corner of the desk, obviously poised to look suave and debonair.

"Mr. Schend." Angel crossed the small office. "I'm sorry to keep you waiting. I had to—" He looked at Cordelia for help, realizing she'd probably given Schend some excuse.

"I explained to Mr. Schend that you were taking the cappuccino machine to the repair shop," Cordelia explained, "and that was why we got stuck with this miserable loaner." She jerked her head in disgust at the coffeepot.

"Okay."

Standing behind Schend, Doyle rolled his eyes.

"Your name is Angel," Schend said. "Angel what? Or is Angel a surname?"

"It's just Angel."

Schend smiled a little, but the nervousness he obviously felt took a lot of the enthusiasm out of it. "A private eye with one name kind of fits into this town, doesn't it?"

"I guess so. What can I do for you, Mr. Schend?"

"Call me Gunnar. Everybody does."

"Sure."

"Detective Kate Lockley at the Los Angeles Police Department seems to hold you in high regard," Schend said. "She recommended that I come see you."

"I'll have to thank her for that." Angel watched

as Cordelia quietly turned the monitor around so that Schend could see it more easily. "Maybe we could talk in my office."

"Sure."

"Hey," Cordelia said, "I took the liberty of sending out for Starbucks."

Angel led the way to the back office and walked behind the desk, waiting for Schend to take his seat.

The television producer gazed around the room in surprise. "Wow, you really go all out when you want to make an impression."

Angel sat as Schend did, not knowing exactly how to take the statement.

"When Detective Lockley told me you'd located your business here, I was really surprised," Schend admitted. "Then when Ms. Chase explained that you were cultivating the seedy Hollywood detective image on purpose, it made sense."

"It did?" Angel asked, trying to find the chain of logic in there somewhere.

"Yeah. I totally understand. It's this town. Everybody's gotta have an angle, make them rise above the rest of the crowd. For you, it's portraying the no-holds-barred kind of detective Humphrey Bogart made famous as Sam Spade and Philip Marlowe."

Angel took that in without saying anything.

"See? Tight-lipped, earnest. I like that approach." Schend glanced around again, then touched the pile of old books beside the phone on the desk. "Everybody's getting their information online, listening to books on CD, or not bothering to read at all, and you're giving the impression you're still researching by hand. That's another good touch." He picked up the top book and read the title outloud. *"The Pathology and Provocation of Demons.* Now, there's a title you don't see a lot of."

"I have some eclectic tastes when it comes to reading material," Angel explained.

Schend put the book back on the stack. "Demon-hunting?"

"It's a study of the origins of demons up to, at the time of writing, the witch hunts that took place in Europe and the United States."

Schend stroked the patch of whiskers on his chin. "A period piece with killer costumes would be an eye-opener. What about the Inquisition? That was going on around then, wasn't it?"

"Yes."

"Now, there's a set of villains for you. Guys could be as memorable as the stormtroopers in *Star Wars.*"

"Knock, knock." Cordelia entered the room with a carryout tray from Starbucks.

Schend accepted the cup she offered, and asked, "How much do you believe in the supernatural, Angel?"

Angel paused, wondering about the television producer's angle. "Maybe a little more than most."

Cordelia sat on one corner of the desk, ignoring the small look of irritation Angel sent her way.

"Most people believe in angels," Schend said. "Do you?"

Angel nodded.

"What about vampires?" Schend asked. "Do you believe in them?"

"They're part of the tapestry of myth."

"So you believe in them?"

"As much as I can."

Schend sipped his cappuccino. "Do you believe Whitney is a vampire?"

An image of the television star filled Angel's mind, but the memory of the young swordswoman intertwined. "No."

"There are a few who do."

Cordelia crossed her arms over her breasts. "Well, that's just stupid. Anyone can see that she's not a vampire."

"Really?" Schend asked. "How?"

"I mean they can *see* it," Cordelia replied. "Take the show that was on tonight. I counted four separate occasions that Whitney Tyler—as Honor

Blaze, radio shock jock—checked her appearance in mirrors and glass windows."

"Well," Schend said defensively, "we didn't want our viewers to forget that first and foremost Honor is a woman."

Ouch, Angel thought, then realized Cordelia would probably agree with the logic.

"Trust me," Doyle said, lounging in the office doorway, "with a bod like that, none of your male audience is going to forget."

"We put the little touches like the makeup and hair checks in there for the female audience," Schend said. "We're drawing heavy numbers from both camps. Demographics are a huge thing when you start hunting sponsors for a show."

"The thing is," Cordelia said, "everyone knows a vampire doesn't cast a reflection in a mirror, or a glass pane."

"We decided to disregard that for the show," Schend said, "after the pilot had been shot and we didn't think about all the times Whitney appeared reflected in windows, a swimming pool, bottles. It would have meant a lot of reshooting."

"Mr. Schend," Angel said.

"Gunnar."

Angel nodded. "Gunnar. Why did you ask if I believed Whitney is a vampire?"

"As I said, there are a lot of people out there

who do," the television executive answered. "But some of them are trying to kill her."

"You mean, they really believe her character is a vampire?"

Angel saw amazement and disbelief in Cordelia's face.

"No. I mean they believe Whitney is actually a vampire working in Hollywood." Schend grinned and shook his head. "If things weren't so screwed up, I don't think I could have been happier. *Dark Midnight* has gone international in its first season. Sure, other shows have done that, but we think we're really going to set new records here. Bootleg copies of episodes are creeping across the Canadian and Mexican borders, and even jumping off from there to the European and Asian markets. I've heard everybody has got some kind of rip-off scheduled to come out for the fall season, but all that's doing is whetting the appetite for the original."

Angel listened quietly, knowing from experience that despite the confident air Schend had, the man was more nervous than he wanted to let on.

"There are hundreds," Schend went on, "maybe thousands of fans out there who are walking around living the vampire lifestyle because of Whitney's character. Staying in during the day and living their lives at night. But the problem here is that some of the viewers who believe Whitney really is a vampire have also tried to stake her."

"Why?" Angel asked.

"Because a stake through the heart is supposed to kill a vampire."

"No, I mean why would they want to kill her?"

"Personally, I think it's because she's become such a celebrity. The guy who shot Lennon is going to live forever. But there are others who think that Whitney represents some kind of vampire conspiracy out to take over Hollywood, then the rest of the world."

"What else has happened?" Angel asked.

"Another guy tried to kill Whitney tonight," Schend responded. He told them about the highway attempt that had happened only hours ago.

"The guy who attacked her is still alive?" Doyle asked.

Schend nodded. "It's a totally whacked-out situation. According to the cop who took this guy down, the guy was like a machine, inhuman."

"Has this guy made any kind of statement?" Angel asked.

"No," Schend replied.

"Where is Whitney now?" Angel asked.

"Safe," Schend said. "She's got an apartment here in L.A. that no one knows about."

"It's not the same one where Tobin Calhoun was killed, is it?" Doyle asked.

"No. We took her out of there that day."

Angel looked a question at Doyle, who quickly explained the Calhoun connection. "No one ever found out anything about Calhoun's death?" Angel asked when Doyle finished his summation.

Schend shook his head. "The police investigated. I think Detective Lockley was involved in that. No one knew if Calhoun was actually the intended victim. With the craziness going on around Whitney now, the detectives working the case are starting to wonder if there was some kind of tie to her."

"Why?" Angel asked.

"I don't know. Maybe it's just a new way of looking at things."

Angel let the silence settle between them for a moment as he gathered his thoughts. His own instincts about the situation warned him away from the case. Whatever was involved, he knew it wasn't going to be easy. But redemption wasn't easy; that was the whole nature of the thing. Redemption cost.

"We've scheduled Whitney for day interviews," Schend said. "But no one seems to care. These people believe what they want to believe. The letters we've gotten at the studio suggested that the daylight appearances were manipulated by computer graphics, or that the person wasn't Whitney at all. Some of the more dedicated followers of the show even objected, saying that seeing Whitney in the daylight made it harder to believe in her on the show. Looking back on it, I think maybe we made a mistake in the beginning."

"What mistake?" Angel asked.

"In the beginning we thought it would be a cool idea if Whitney made it a habit of only agreeing to interviews at night. Kind of add to the mystery of the show and her. Leno and Letterman agreed to shoot special interview spots for their shows that made it obvious they were filmed at night. So did Conan, *Entertainment Tonight*, and MTV. Even CNN did coverage on the show with a nighttime shoot."

"But it just lent to the madness," Doyle said.

"Exactly. Whitney's got a lot of fans in city hall and the legislature. The Wolfram and Hart law firm has even represented us in shooting-site acquisitions and handled overseas licensing in some tricky negotiations."

Wolfram & Hart, Angel knew from experience and past dealings, was one of—if not *the*—most high-powered law firms in L.A. However, the firm was also involved in some of the most illegal and evil dealings in the city. It stood to reason that maybe they handled legitimate business as well. But the name still increased the vague unease Angel felt.

"The police weren't able to help you?" Angel asked.

"They're convinced that the loony tunes crawling out of the woodwork with nothing more on their little brains than staking Whitney as a vampire were solitary instances. No overall conspiracy theory."

"But you feel differently?"

"Angel, let's get something straight. Mano-to-mano." Schend sighed. "Whitney is not only my friend, but she's the biggest cash cow I've ever had my hands on. I don't want to see her hurt. So far the police have found no connection between the first two guys they busted for attacking Whitney. They tell me they're not exactly hopeful on this third guy. He's something of a cipher. No name. Fingerprints aren't on file."

"That takes time," Angel pointed out.

"Sure. I understand that. After the latest attack, I called Detective Lockley because she impressed me during the investigation of the first two guys. She suggested I give you a call. She told me you have a certain talent for weird cases, and you were a guy who'd stick, not turn tail when the going got a little rough."

"And you expect the going to get rough?"

"The first two guys?" Schend said. "They came at Whitney on the studio lot and got put down by security guards. This last guy drove a freakin' truck through a diner full of people to get to her. What do you think the odds are?"

The shrill blast of Schend's cell phone shattered the silence in the office. The television executive took the handset from inside his motorcycle jacket.

"Gunnar." He waited for just a moment, eyes wide and growing wider, listening to the excited speaker on the other end of the phone. "I'll be right there." He put the handset away and stood. "That was the relief guard stationed at Whitney's apartment. He said the guy he was supposed to relieve is dead and Whitney's missing. I've got to get over there." He headed for the door.

Angel stood. "Gunnar."

Schend turned, looking totally stressed.

"What's the address?" Angel asked.

"Where's Gunnar?" Angel hurried through the apartment building's foyer. A half-dozen people sat scattered in the various chairs and sofas, overflow from the bar where the night's business was winding down.

"Parking the Hummer in the private garage," Cordelia said. "It's new and he didn't want to leave it out."

"Nice to see that he has his priorities straight." Angel ran the swipe card the television producer had given him through the reader beside the elevator. The doors opened with a *ding!*

"You ask me," Doyle said, "I think he's just afraid to go up there."

"No one did," Cordelia retorted.

"Did what?" Doyle asked.

"Ask you." Cordelia stepped into the elevator cage with Angel. "Personally, I can understand why he's taking care of the car. I know all about the status-symbol envy people can have. Especially the status-impaired ones."

"What floor, sir?" the elevator operator asked. He was shaved bald and looked big enough to bench-press Volkswagens. He wore a blue blazer with corduroy patches and tan khakis.

"Eight," Angel replied.

"If you'll just swipe the card, sir." The man pointed to the reader inside the cage.

Angel did and the elevator doors closed. The cage started up smoothly. His stomach tightened a little more.

"First visit?" the elevator operator asked.

"Yes."

"You didn't look like you were from the neighborhood."

"No."

"You'll want to be quiet this time of night," the elevator operator said. "Our residents appreciate the environment we're able to give them."

"Sure." Angel watched the floor indicator. So far it seemed as if Schend's security man had been able to keep the murder quiet. His participation wasn't going to set well with Lockley afterward, and he felt kind of bad about that since she'd recommended him.

The elevator door opened on the eighth floor.

Angel stepped out and headed to the right, scouring the hallway for any signs of the violence that had been done in Whitney Tyler's apartment. The scent of fresh blood brushed his nostrils, too faint for anyone human to scent, awakening the hunger that he lived with every day. He stopped at the door to Whitney's apartment and knocked.

"Who is it?" a man's tense voice asked.

"Angel. Gunnar was supposed to call."

"He did. Wait just a sec." Locks rattled for a moment, then the door opened. The security guard was in his mid-twenties, pale, with eyes too closely set, and nervous. He pushed the door closed and unfastened the security chain. "Come on in. It's creepy being here with a dead guy you used to know. This job, they never said anything about anything like this."

Angel stepped into the room. The blood scent grew stronger. "Where is the body?"

"Bedroom." The guard pointed.

The apartment was spacious, comfortably equipped with plush furniture that suggested pre-arranged pieces rather than personal choices. Monet prints hung on the strawberry cream pastel walls. The room had been tastefully decorated, a home away from home for someone wealthy enough to afford it. But that had been before tonight's visit.

Messages had been spray-painted on the walls. TIME TO DIE! YOU CANNOT ESCAPE! PENANCE MUST BE DEALT! EVIL HAS NO PLACE ON THIS EARTH! ABOMINATIONS WILL BE DESTROYED! REPENT AND RECANT! PUNISH THE GUILTY!

The messages had been written over and over. Padding from the slashed furniture littered the carpet where huge pieces had been carved away. Glass shards from the Tiffany lamps and glass-topped coffee table gleamed.

The blood trail started in the bedroom doorway.

Cautiously, his senses alive to every movement and sound around him, Angel entered the room. He glanced at Doyle, knowing the half-demon's senses were as sharp as his own. "Do you smell anything?"

"Only the blood. And the dead man."

The dead man hung from the ceiling fan fixture overhead, a belt tight around his neck. Blood stained his chest all the way to his groin from his slashed throat. The ceiling fan creaked threateningly, starting to slowly turn the dead body around. The arms and legs quivered as the halting motor struggled with the huge burden placed on it.

The bedroom was like the living room, carefully furnished and equipped with prints as well as ceramic statues of angels. Someone had gone through all the ceramic angels and broken the wings off.

Angel found the light switches on the wall and turned the fan off. The body swayed drunkenly.

Crossing the room, Angel pushed the bathroom door open, then followed it inside. When he flicked the light on, he scanned the separate bath and shower cubicles. The spray-paint messages continued on the bathroom walls, the same apparent litany over and over. Only this time the dead guard's blood was an added ingredient.

Angel surveyed the wreckage of cosmetics and toiletries strewn across the two sinks. Writing marred the mirror so badly it was hard to see Doyle's reflection when he stepped into the room. Angel's own reflection wasn't there.

PURGATORY AWAITS was spelled out on the glass doors on the mirrored shower unit, reflected in the mirrors above the sinks till it looked like an unending proclamation plunging down into a no-man's land of reflections.

"Doesn't exactly exude that homey feeling, does it?" Doyle asked.

"No. But this couldn't have been done in just minutes." Angel stepped back into the bedroom, spotting all the threatening graffiti on the walls there as well.

"Well," Doyle said, "at least, it couldn't have been done in minutes by anything human."

"Does this look supernatural to you?" Angel studied the corpse. In addition to the slashes covering his throat, the guard had an indentation the size of a baseball in his left temple.

"It's got a certain whang about it." Doyle approached the corpse. "Never even got his pistol out of the holster."

"Someone smashed his skull in. The slashes across his throat were just to finish the job."

"What about the woman?"

Angel looked at the bed. It was still neatly arranged, pristine white bedcovers neatly in place; an island of perfection in a sea of chaos. "I don't know. Maybe she wasn't here."

"Her guard is here. I don't think Gunnar would be in much of a mood for them to let her walk around untended."

"I know."

"Where is she?"

Turning, Angel found Gunnar Schend standing in the bedroom doorway. "She's not here."

Schend's eyes focused on the dead man. "Then they have kidnapped her!" The producer turned and stared back into the large living room.

"Actually, I believe Whitney wasn't abducted."

"What?"

"The graffiti," Angel explained. "It's a series of threats. Promised persecution and vengeance. If someone had taken Whitney, they wouldn't have made those. From the look of things, I think they would have killed her if they'd gotten their hands on her."

"God," Schend whispered. "I knew these people were crazy, but I didn't know they were this crazy."

"The good news is that she's probably still alive," Angel pointed out. "If they don't catch her, she'll probably be in touch. She's probably just scared."

"Okay." Schend took a deep, calming breath. "Okay. What do we do?"

"When we leave, you call the police," Angel said.

"Are you kidding? Do you know what kind of publicity—" Schend stopped speaking, then reached for the cell phone in his jacket. "Of course. You're right. I'll call them. They tape all the incoming nine-one-

one calls, right? I've seen them played back on television."

"Skip nine-one-one this time," Angel said. "They've also got reporters tied into those lines. Police investigators are one thing, but having reporters crawling all over this apartment right now is positively scary. Call Lockley. She may be on. If not, try for another detective."

"I don't have her number."

Angel recited it from memory.

"With something like this, we need to make a public statement within minutes. Lockley may succeed in keeping the media out of this for the moment, but she's not going to keep them away forever."

Angel nodded and got Schend moving toward the apartment door. "Doyle, this apartment building has security cameras everywhere. Why don't you and Cordelia see if you can find the security office and get a look at the tapes. Lockley will probably have her people do the same thing, but they won't be as generous."

"On my way," Doyle said. He went to the doorway and gathered Cordelia, who seemed happy enough to leave the apartment.

"Is there somewhere else Whitney would go?" Angel asked.

"You mean if she wasn't kidnapped?" Schend asked.

Angel nodded.

"I don't know. She'd call me first." Schend wiped his face. "She'd call me if there was any trouble."

"Cell phones aren't always reliable. Maybe she left a message at home." Angel read through the messages on the walls again, trying to determine if there was something he was missing. *If there is, I'm still missing it.*

"I tried there on the way over," Schend assured him. "There were no messages."

"Are either of these security guards new?" Angel asked.

"No. Everybody ever assigned to Whitney was cleared through my offices."

"You cleared them?"

"No. I've got an assistant who does that. She's very good at what she does."

"So you've seen these men before?"

"Yeah." Schend peered at the other security guard by the door. "At least, I think I have. You don't exactly get on talking terms with security people."

The door opened, and a woman's shocked voice demanded, "Who is this?"

Stunned, Schend turned and looked at the woman in the doorway.

Angel gazed at her. With the rich red-gold hair and those features, there was no mistaking

Whitney Tyler. She wore a charcoal jacket over a dark green turtleneck, black jeans, and calf-high stiletto heeled boots.

"Whitney!" Schend shouted. "You're alive!"

Whitney stepped into the room with a shopping bag in her hands. She gazed in shock around the room, taking in the damage. "Another one of those crazies found me, didn't he?"

"We don't know what happened," Schend said, approaching her and taking her into his arms. "God, I'm just glad you're all right."

Whitney pushed herself from the producer's embrace. "I can't keep working like this, Gunnar. We need to put the show on hiatus until we figure out a way to make me safe."

"You're going to be safe," Schend promised. "Look, I went out tonight and found someone who can help us. This is Angel. He's a private detective. I've been told he's the best at this kind of thing."

Angel stared into the gray-green eyes that locked with his. His stomach turned cold and spun, and he could almost hear the crash of waves in the background.

Whitney gazed deep into his eyes for a moment, then smiled perplexedly. "Do we know each other?"

CHAPTER SEVEN

Clifden, Ireland, 1758

"Brooding again?" Darla asked.

Angelus glanced up at the woman. "I haven't finished from last time." He sat at a back table in Danann's Tavern, a small place only a couple streets up from the docks.

Whale-oil lanterns flickered on the walls, and a large wheel near the top of the room held a couple dozen tapers that occasionally dripped hot wax onto inattentive guests passing by below. The tavern was a dive, a place where illegal business was done and dockworkers came to drink cheap grog and look at women.

Mismatched tables and chairs filled the center floor, and a roaring fire in the huge fireplace beat back the night's chill. One of the serving girls turned the handle on the spit near the flames, the seared flesh of the animal shining with grease.

Darla wore a scarlet dress that clung to her figure and revealed the creamy white tops of her breasts. "I wish you'd stop thinking about that woman."

"Ripping her heart out with my bare hands is a pleasant thought."

Darla pulled out a nearby chair and sat. Angelus noticed several pairs of eyes belonging to the dockworkers in the room seemed to come naturally to Darla.

"She's dead," Darla said.

"It would have felt better if I had killed her myself." Before he could continue, they were interrupted by Darius striding up to address them.

"Ah, me little lovebirds." Darius made his way over to them, a tin cup brimming with good Irish whiskey. "So here ye are."

"Hello, Darius," Darla said. "You're enjoying your ill-gotten gain, I see."

"Oh, and thoroughly, woman. Never let it be said that Captain Darius didn't know how to properly fritter away his wealth in high-minded fashion." Darius's eyes flamed red from the drinking he'd been doing. His rolling gait seemed a little more pronounced, and his gestures were broad and expansive.

Since returning to Clifden, Darius had negotiated the sales of the weapons *Handsome Jack* had carried. The vampire captain had bemoaned the fact that the Scots activists he'd sold the arms to had been poorer than church mice, but he'd taken their money and wished them well all the same. They'd abandoned *Lugh's Fancy,* casting the ship free out onto the sea.

"Is that a new dress I see ye a-wearing?" Darius pulled a chair up to the table and sat.

"Yes." Darla preened.

Darius chuckled. "I see ye've not been letting yer share lay idle."

"Money comes and goes," Darla said. "I have no problems enjoying it."

Darius looked at Angelus. "And ye, my pirate-in-the-making, what have ye done with yer share?"

"Nothing," Angelus said.

"He's been moping over his new scars," Darla said.

"Ah, lad"—Darius clapped Angelus on the shoulder—"a proper pirate should be a fearsome man, one whose mere bloodthirsty look should make even brave men quail." He smiled.

Angelus barely bottled the black rage that filled him. Darius didn't know him well enough to take those kinds of liberties.

"Don't ye worry yer knob overmuch about yer

looks," Darius advised. "A way to a woman's loving arms isn't through looks. It's through how much silver and gold ye can cross her palm with. Trust ol' Cap'n Darius on that."

Footsteps sounded on the warped boardwalk in front of Danann's Tavern. The way they thumped rhythmically against the wooden slats with strong cadence drew Angelus's attention instantly.

"Soldiers," Darla stated, gazing toward the front door. An uncertain smile lighted her lips. "This should be interesting."

"I've heard that the king's guard have been looking for the arms shipment what went missing," Darius said. "But they're afraid of looking too far outside of Clifden proper in the event they happen upon a group of overbrave Scots with quick fingers and the eyes of fisherhawks."

The front door opened, and a young giant filled the doorway. He stood over six feet tall, and his shoulders barely fit through the door. His black clothes and traveling cloak held road grit, and even across the room Angelus could smell the stench of horses and wood smoke on him.

"They're not from the city," Angelus stated quietly. Apprehension filled his stomach with sour bile. He shifted in his chair and pushed his coat back from the sword belted at his side. Now that he was no longer playing pirate, he'd traded the cutlass for a short sword of good German steel that he was much more familiar with.

The young giant strode into the room. Most of the dockworkers and sailors who'd come into the tavern for a meal and drink instantly rounded their shoulders and did their best to turn invisible.

Five more young men, hard-eyed and grim-featured, stepped into the room after their leader. Despite the road dust and stench of horses that clung to them, all the young men were clean-shaven. They'd been on the road for a long time, but they'd tended to their personal appearances.

"Now, there's a handsome man," Darla said in a soft voice.

"Now, there's a dangerous man," Darius stated hollowly. "And him on a mission, too, from the looks of him." The captain put his cup to one side, and the drunken behavior dropped away. His hand strayed down to the sword at his side.

"I am Fiachra O'Domhnallain of the Clan Bresail, once from Galway as my ancestors were," the young giant declared fiercely. "I come here this night to set right a wrong, and to end an evil pestilence that steadily claims the lives of the unsuspecting. My hand will not be stayed, and I promise no mercy to those who number among my foes, only a quick death as is the Lord's judgment against all things foul."

"Bit of a braggart, ain't he?" Darius asked.

Angelus said nothing. The dark part of him that stayed eternally hungry these days welcomed the coming battle. He smiled.

"A ship was taken by carrion creatures a fortnight ago," O'Domhnallain stated. "People protected by the Crown and by the Church were killed, and property was taken. Those guilty will be put to death." He reached under his traveling cloak and took out a silver cross nearly a foot tall, ending in a sharp point at the foot. The cross was worth a fortune. He flicked his arm back, throwing the cross toward the doorway.

The cross twinkled in the lantern light as it spun, then embedded in the wooden frame above the doorway with a loud *thunk!*

O'Domhnallain pulled a long sword from beneath his cloak. "Those who pass from this tavern," he challenged fiercely, "shall do so on bended knee beneath the symbol of our God who died for our sins that we might live forever. Those whom are shunned by the Lord shall be turned from the door and made unable to pass by the evil that has swallowed their souls."

The men behind O'Domhnallain spread out, drawing weapons as well as wooden stakes.

"Come forth now," O'Domhnallain ordered, "or we shall come upon you and ask no questions. All that remain within this room shall die."

Immediately the dockworkers and sailors among the tavern crowd went forward. They dropped to their knees and knee-walked toward the door.

"Turn your faces up to the cross," O'Domhnallain commanded harshly. "Acknowledge the debt you owe for the love and tender mercy that you were given."

The sailors and dockworkers continued through the door unmolested. The small group in the tavern emptied quickly, and it became quickly apparent who wasn't leaving.

"Well," Darius said, "I should suppose this promises to be a bonny fray." He stood up and bared his sword with a hiss of steel on leather. He raised his voice. "Boy."

O'Domhnallain stared at him, pale eyes as cold as ice.

Darius spat on the floor. "Our kind is already restricted to the night's shadows, ever wary in the true light of day. I'll not be driven from an Irish drinking establishment by a pack of curs with lofty ideals."

"You are not human," the young giant accused.

Darius's grin split his whiskered face. "I'm more than human, boy. More than you'll ever be no matter how fiercely you believe."

"Moira," O'Domhnallain called.

The woman was dressed as the other men in her

company were. Her sword was naked steel in her fist.

She can't be alive! But Angelus looked at her and knew it was true. Despite the fact that he'd broken one of her arms and pulled the other out of joint and watched her go down with *Handsome Jack*, the young woman lived. More than that, she appeared to be no worse for the wear.

"Are these the men who attacked the ship you guarded?" O'Domhnallain demanded.

Moira gazed around the room at the vampires that had made up Darius's crew. She locked those fiery gray-green eyes on Angelus. "Yes. And I would never forget this one. He is the most evil of them all."

CHAPTER EIGHT

Angel stared into the depths of Whitney Tyler's gray-green eyes and tried to get over the uncanny resemblance. "No. We don't know each other."

"I could swear I've seen you somewhere before."

"Maybe," Angel suggested softly, "I remind you of someone else."

Her eyes continued to study his face for a moment. "Maybe." She turned to Schend. "Did you catch whoever did this?"

"No."

Whitney put the shopping bag on the floor. "Did the security guy ever get here?"

"You never saw him?" Schend asked.

"No. I sat and waited till I thought I was going to go crazy. That whole scene at the diner, with the truck and all that, was just too much. I couldn't take sitting here by myself, so I went to the Quik-Shop and grabbed munchies."

"You shouldn't have left the apartment," Schend said.

Whitney glanced around the apartment. "You're right. I should have stayed here so the guy who did this could have practiced on me instead of the walls." She turned back to Schend. "Besides which, you can't exactly send out for Cheese Doodles and strawberry yogurt."

"How long have you been gone?" Angel asked.

Shrugging, Whitney replied. "Maybe thirty, forty-five minutes."

"How long did you wait on the security guard to arrive?"

"About an hour."

"He didn't call to say he was late?"

"No." Whitney's attention wandered to the bedroom door. Her eyes focused on the crimson smear in the doorway. In the next instant she was in motion. "What's going on?"

Angel took her by the elbow, halting her.

"Ow." Whitney yanked her elbow away. "That's quite a grip you've got there."

"Sorry," Angel apologized. For just an instant he'd been back on *Handsome Jack,* the salty scent of the sea and fresh blood mixed with spent gunpowder hanging in the air. "You don't want to go in there."

"Why?"

"The late security guard," Schend explained tensely, "really is the *late* security guard now."

Stubbornly Whitney walked to the door, carefully avoiding the blood smeared in the doorway. Then she stopped, frozen in her tracks. She wrapped her arms around her stomach as if she'd just been hit. "Oh, my god," she whispered. Her confidence eroded and tears tracked down her face.

Doyle stared at the images on the security computer monitor, watching the tapes roll through the last couple hours. Watching them in fast-forward was no real strain because there hadn't been that much activity during the night.

The security room was hardly bigger than a good-sized closet. Filled with computer and surveillance equipment, the addition of Doyle and Cordelia to Todd, the uniformed security guard on duty, made for a tight fit.

"There's Whitney Tyler arriving again," Cordelia said.

Doyle watched the woman cross the screen in the apartment building's main foyer. They'd seen the tape twice before. He checked the time/date stamp in the upper right hand corner. For the third time Whitney consistently arrived at the apartment building at 1:17 A.M. Wednesday morning. It was 3:34 A.M. now.

"Doesn't she look heavier than she did on tonight's episode?" Cordelia asked.

Doyle looked at the woman with increased interest. Cordelia had accused him of gawking earlier. Actually, it was hard not to gawk. For a woman who'd been run off the highway, nearly run down and staked by a rampaging madman, Whitney Tyler had cleaned up very well.

"It's the security tape," Todd said. He was big, slightly overweight, with straw-colored hair and a round face. A package of Snickers bite-size candies lay open on the desk. "Those cameras aren't very flattering. You get that overweight look from the fish-eye lenses we use."

Personally, Doyle thought Whitney looked fantastic. Maybe a little tired, but after having watched some maniac drive a big truck through a diner wall only a few hours ago, that look was probably normal. But she also caused an uncomfortable itch in the back of his mind.

"I think she looks a little heavier," Cordelia said as Whitney stepped into the elevator. "With that hem design, she could get away with it. Maybe success is going to her head *and* her hips."

The camera footage changed when the security guard tapped the keyboard. Todd had cut and pasted the video footage into a file for them, adding all the different views so it looked as if the camera was deliberately following the woman. The new view showed the interior of the elevator cage. The view changed again when she stepped from the elevator, picking her up as she walked down the hallway toward her apartment.

"Do you have cameras inside the rooms?" Doyle asked.

"No way," Todd answered quickly. "We're talking about invasion of privacy as well as Peeping Tom laws. Get caught doing that, and you're in lockup with real sickos." He tapped the keyboard again. "I've added in the additional footage of Ms. Tyler arriving at the apartment building a few minutes ago. Want to see it, too?"

"Yeah." Doyle watched as Whitney walked through the foyer again. The return trip to her apartment was just as uneventful as the first time he'd seen it.

There'd been no homicidal maniacs and only a handful of people who'd gotten off on Whitney Tyler's floor other than the security guards, one of whom was now hanging from the ceiling fan in her bedroom.

"Can I get a copy of the tape?" Doyle asked.

"Why?" Todd asked. "It doesn't sound like you found anything you were looking for."

"Maybe I'll give it a go again later. See something I didn't see the first time."

"Look, I'd like to help you out, but I could get into some heavy trouble for doing something like that."

"We won't tell," Cordelia promised.

"Sure, and the next thing I know, I'm being credited as a source on *A Current Affair* or something."

"That'll never happen," Doyle said earnestly.

"I wouldn't do it for less than fifty bucks," Todd replied. "Cash. On the barrelhead. No IOUs." He turned back to the keyboard.

Cordelia shoved her way by him. "Todd," she said in a low voice.

Todd's attention perked up at once. He smiled. "Yes?"

"I was thinking there might be something else you'd be interested in."

Todd leaned back in the chair and grinned wolfishly. "And what might that be?"

"A phone number," Cordelia said. She took a business card from her pocketbook.

"Yours?"

"You can reach me there." Cordelia smiled invitingly.

Todd only thought about it for a moment, then took down a blank compact VHS tape and shoved it into the recorder. It duplicated in minutes. "It's all digital," he said when it finished, "so you shouldn't have any problems with it." He offered the tape and snatched the business card from Cordelia's hand.

"Thanks, Todd." Cordelia led the way out of the security room.

"That was going a little above and beyond the call of duty, don't you think?" Doyle asked as they walked to the elevator. "I mean, it's good of you to do, but there's no telling how much that little creep is going to be calling."

Cordelia raised her eyebrows. "You seriously think I gave him my number?"

"You didn't?"

"No."

"Then whose—"

"That card," Cordelia informed him, "has my old stylist's number on it. After what he did to my hair, you don't think I'm going there anymore, do you?"

"The first thing you're going to do is talk to the police," Angel said.

Whitney had recovered some of her composure. "Can't we just leave?"

"No. There's been a murder."

"I know." Whitney hugged herself more tightly, pacing through the wreckage of the living room.

"And the guy who did it may come back at any time."

"I don't think so," Angel said. He couldn't help being captivated by the way she looked. She resembled the swordswoman so much it was almost unbelievable. It helped that he had seen unbelievable things before; in fact, he even *was* something unbelievable. But the fear that filled her was something he just simply couldn't imagine in that woman in Galway.

"If he does," Schend said, "Angel's here now. He knows how to handle things like this. Probably just pull out his gun and start blasting away."

"I don't carry a pistol," Angel said.

Schend gaped at him.

Angel shrugged. "I don't need one."

"My god, man. That security guard in there was bigger than you *and* he carried a gun."

"Yeah," Angel said. "You can see how much that helped him."

Cordelia knocked on the door, then entered with Doyle at her heels when the guard let them in.

"The security tapes?" Angel asked hopefully.

"If the guy came in through the main foyer," Cordelia said, "he wasn't wearing a sign."

"But," Doyle added, lifting a cassette tape, "we got a copy of the footage to review later."

Angel nodded, turning his attention to Whitney.

"After the police cut you loose, we've got to find a safe place for you until we figure out what to do next."

"We've got an on-location shoot downtown later today," Schend said.

"No," Whitney objected. "Gunnar, a man just got killed in my bedroom tonight."

"Whitney, I know," the television producer said, "but Tomas spent weeks setting this shoot up through the L.A. Chamber of Commerce. It's now or never for this episode."

"We can do the shoot in the studio," Whitney said. "Just restructure the scene."

Schend shook his head. "No can do. You know part of the package we sell with this series is this city. If we start missing those, *Dark Midnight* is going to look like every other action-adventure show out there. We have to do this."

"It's going to be kind of hard to do if I'm dead, too."

Schend obviously didn't have an argument for that. He threw his hands up in surrender.

"We'll worry about that later," Angel suggested. "Right now, just get through the police investigation."

"I've gotten two other cards with that symbol on it," Whitney said, gazing at the reproduction Angel had drawn.

Angel tapped the paper napkin he'd drawn the symbol on and looked at Whitney. "This exact symbol?"

"I believe so. Both times my apartments before were trashed, there were index cards left behind. Gunnar knows more about them."

Angel leaned back in his chair. They'd retreated to his office as soon as the police had cut Schend and Whitney loose.

"Actually, I don't know much," Schend admitted. "That symbol looks like Greek to me."

"I thought it looked more like Farsi," Angel said. "With all the curlicues and dots."

"I've had the show's writers and researchers try to figure out what that symbol means. A couple of them think it has some historical meaning, but they couldn't find out what."

"Maybe I could take it around and ask a few questions," Doyle suggested.

"I'm telling you you're wasting your time," Schend said. "The people I use on the show are good."

"Your people probably don't have the resources I do."

"What does the other part mean?" Cordelia asked. "*Atonement?* What's supposed to be atoned for?"

"A crime, maybe," Angel said, glancing at Whitney.

Whitney shook her head. "If you consider parking tickets and speeding infractions worth killing someone over, then I'm guilty. But there hasn't been anything else."

Angel studied the symbol he'd drawn on the paper napkin. It was all confusing; Doyle's vision, Angel's memories suddenly surfacing as well as the symbol. He felt that he should know the symbol, but he didn't.

Whitney shivered suddenly and rubbed her arms briskly.

"Cold?" Doyle asked.

"No. I just realized that we've gone from stalker to killer. Not exactly the upgrade you'd want in your life."

Schend spoke up. "Look, we're going to have to talk about damage control here. With the police in your apartment and a dead guy on his way out, the media is going to be all over this. Sponsors are going to get nervous. That's another reason the on-location spot tomorrow—today—is so important. If we start choking on our schedule, they're going to think we're hiding something."

"We will be," Whitney responded. "Me. Don't you get it, Gunnar? You might as well be putting me to bed every night in a Venus's-flytrap if we continue shooting."

"Do you have somewhere else you can go?" Angel asked. "Someplace safe?"

The question took some of the anger from Whitney. "No."

"You can spend the night here," Angel offered. "Until we can work something else out."

"Thank you."

"Whitney," Schend said patiently, "that show is the only protection you have. It makes the money that allows you to live the way you want, and hide. If you disappear and leave this season in the lurch, I can guarantee you the money will dry up in a heartbeat."

"Are you threatening me, Gunnar?" An angry flush colored Whitney's face.

"No," Schend replied. "I'm just trying to help you think this thing through. Before you jump off the deep end and we can't save the show or you."

"Who's thinking about pulling back off the show?" Whitney asked.

"Davis Hollings for one."

"Personally, I wouldn't mind seeing Hollings go," Whitney said. "He's a creep. He doesn't know how to take no for an answer."

"*Professionally*, you'd hate to see him go. Hollings and NewNet underwrite fifteen percent of the show."

"That's because we deliver him the young audience who uses his company's search engine," Whitney replied. "The guy's slime."

"What about Hollings?" Angel said.

"You haven't heard of Hollings or NewNet?" Schend asked.

"Sure," Cordelia spoke up. "Cyber-boy. Created the newest, latest, best net search engine that's attracting geek-boys and geek-girls everywhere, as well as the advertisers who like to sell them stuff. NewNet is supposed to be the 'Next Big Thing' in the world of virtual, and Hollings is the golden child. However, he's got kind of a dark side. He likes television starlets. Eight months ago he nearly got busted for stalking Abby Langtree. I can name four more starlets he chased after before and since, but Abby Langtree was the first who nearly got him into one of those fashionable orange jumpsuits all the convicts are into."

"You've had problems with Hollings?" Angel asked Whitney.

"Nothing we couldn't handle tactfully," Schend assured.

" 'Tactfully' isn't what I would call it," Whitney replied disgustedly. "Hollings has stalked me a few times, hired a couple guys to steal some of my . . . *personal* things, and used his position as the show's major sponsor to set up dinners and casual dates. Those few dates have been anything but casual. If I hadn't learned martial arts for the show, I wouldn't have been able to defend myself."

"Now, there's a suspect," Cordelia said. "Have you checked into Davis Hollings?"

Schend continued shredding the paper napkin, obviously not comfortable with the topic. "Davis Hollings isn't exactly the kind of guy you can do that with."

"Translation," Whitney said sarcastically, "the studio is afraid to push Hollings. And they're afraid for me to push him."

"We've tried to arrange it so Whitney is never left alone with him," Schend said. "We've been somewhat successful."

"It's still like being around an octopus with attention deficit hyper activity disorder." Whitney shrugged. "But I have to admit things have been better for the last couple months. He's kept his distance a little better."

"How long ago was the first attack?" Angel asked.

"About three months. After the first one, Hollings offered to put his own security staff around me. And to let me live with him in his private fortress."

Doyle glanced at Angel. They sat at the table in his living quarters after Schend had left and while Cordelia was showing Whitney the bedroom. "What do you think? Hollings gets upset, hires a bunch of thugs to scare the living daylights out of Whitney, then sets himself up to be the hero?"

Angel considered it. "Maybe. Except that everything's gotten extreme. Driving the wrecker through the diner wall was definitely over the top."

"Like you've never seen someone go over the top before because of homicidal and hormonal urges," Doyle pointed out.

"We'll talk to him," Angel agreed. "We'll have Cordelia look into Davis Hollings's background and see what she can find out."

Angel turned his attention to the symbol he'd drawn. The word *atonement* written under the mysterious symbol might not have been put there for her, but for him. The cases that he usually got came from one of Doyle's visions, as this one had, but this one had come with its own baggage, bringing those memories of the swordswoman all those years ago. Maybe the word had been put under the symbol this time to further draw his attention.

He didn't know, but he had the definite impression he was going to find out.

CHAPTER NINE

Clifden, Ireland, 1758

Angelus stared at the young swordswoman at the other end of Danann's Tavern as he rose from his seat at the table.

Over a dozen vampires remained within the tavern, all of them rising to their feet now. They hissed and growled as their faces changed to reveal their true dark natures.

Angelus let his features change as well, feeling more confident as two of O'Domhnallain's men involuntarily took a half-step back. The young giant himself stood firmly behind Moira, who hadn't flinched at all.

"Ye have but six men and a woman among ye," Darius challenged, "and ye dare to come in here and make wartalk."

"You count six men and a woman," O'Domhnallain replied, "but I know our Lord guides our destinies as well. We don't stand alone."

Darius spat onto the floor in front of Moira. "Well, at least ye won't die alone then." He stepped forward, his broad cutlass fisted at his side.

Three crossbow quarrels exploded through the window to Darius's left. Angelus heard the rattle of breaking glass even as he watched two of the quarrels sink deeply into the vampire captain's chest.

Both the quarrels that struck Darius missed his heart. He roared with rage and yanked the wooden shafts from his body, snapping them and dropping them to the floor.

The third quarrel pierced the heart of a vampire standing just behind Darius. The vampire exploded into dust.

"Of course," O'Domhnallain said in a mocking tone, "there are a few more men waiting outside."

"Ye damned cheat!" Darius roared.

"I never claimed to be an honorable man," O'Domhnallain replied. "Only a God-fearing one. Evil knows no honor except as a tool to use against those who recognize the sanctity of life."

"Help me grab that table, laddie." Darius grabbed the table in one hand, gesturing to Angelus to take the other. "We best get that damned window closed." His men surged forward and held the warriors at bay.

More quarrels ripped into the room. One embedded in Darius's back while another pierced Angelus's left arm. Angelus ignored it and lifted the other side of the table.

Darius gave a loud battle cry as they raced across the small tavern and flipped the table so the top would meet the window. Before they had it in place, two quarrels thumped into the tabletop. Grease-stained rags tied around the shafts trailed flames, splashing them across the weathered wood where they burned greedily.

Angelus held the table in place while Darius took a long knife from his boot and slammed it home through the table into the wall above the window. When he finished, the table hung from the knife.

"Now let's have at them," Darius snarled. His eyes gleamed fiery red with madness and bloodlust.

Darla threw a chair at the swordswoman. Moira stood her ground and swung her sword, breaking the chair into pieces. One of the vampire sailors went down with a blade through his heart, but it allowed two more vampires to grab the swordsman and yank him to the ground. Their fangs savaged him, making short work of him. The man's shrill cries of fear died as suddenly as the man himself.

Angelus ripped the bandages from his burned right hand that he might better grip the sword. His blackened flesh cracked and tore, spilling fresh blood.

Three more men charged in through the door to join O'Domhnallain's forces.

There were few real swordsmen among Darius's group. The captain himself was no mean exception, but the others seldom stood their ground for long. Then the three men at the back of the human group drew bottles from their riding cloaks, broke the necks from them, and started shaking the contents over the nearest vampires.

Vampire flesh smoked and sizzled when the liquid touched them.

"Holy water!" one of the stricken vampires screamed, falling back as huge blisters formed on his face and neck.

Darla stripped away the skirted part of her dress, leaving her in the blouse top and drawers, freeing her legs so she could move more easily. She flung the lower part of the dress over the nearest man, covering his head and shoulders. The man struck out blindly, boldly overextending himself.

Moving with almost impossible quickness and knowing hands, Darla seized the man's arm and broke it with a crunch. She tore the sword from his hand, then raised it and cleaved the man from crown to chin while he remained under the dress. Even as the man stumbled and died, Darla pulled him to her to act as a momentary shield from his companions, then drank heavily from the wound.

The young swordswoman advanced on Angelus, her weapon pulled back and poised to strike. Glacial hatred shone in her eyes. She swung.

Angelus parried the blow and returned a thrust of his own that the woman narrowly avoided. They fought in silence for a moment, blades reduced to hissing steel as they found a common battleground among the others.

"I thought you were dead," he said.

"You were wrong, hellbeast."

Even though he knew he'd dislocated her right shoulder, her arm never seemed stronger or surer. He blocked a strike that would have taken both his eyes if it had landed, dodging back quickly and running into one of Darius's crew.

The big vampire held a double-bitted ax that he swung at full strength, roaring the whole time. Moira slid easily under the blade, touching down briefly with one hand splayed before her, then lunging up to shove the metal-sheathed wooden blade through the vampire's heart.

Angelus regained his balance just as the vampire he'd bumped up against turned to dust. The swordswoman charged through the swirling remnants, her swordpoint darting at Angelus again.

Before Angelus could do more than turn, she ran a foot of steel through his stomach. It felt as if his guts had been set on fire. He lifted a foot and kicked her back, causing her to pull the sword from his body.

She rolled and got to her feet, a smile on her face. For a moment her gray-green eyes looked black. She lifted her sword again and came at him relentlessly.

"Who are you?" Angelus demanded as he was driven back.

"I am your final death and your doom," she promised evenly. "I will be your final judgment, hellbeast."

The blade flashed faster and faster, narrowing Angelus's defense till he was no longer totally able to protect himself. The sharp point glided into his flesh again and again, as deftly as a clothier's needle darting a seam. He burned every time she touched him.

"Fire the tavern!" O'Domhnallain reached for one of the whale-oil lanterns hanging on the wall and smashed it against the back wall of the building. Burning oil dug fiery talons into the wood, scorching it instantly. Gray smoke pooled along the ceiling.

Other members of O'Domhnallain's group scattered more lanterns, starting new pools of fire. Then some of the warriors outside grew brave enough to smash the table from the window. Crossbows filled the empty space, throwing quarrels with deadly accuracy across the burning tavern into the vampires.

The swordswoman kept up her attack, but never saw Darla come up behind her. Darla had a flintlock pistol in one hand, obviously taken from one of the vampire pirates. She used both hands to aim and cock the weapon, holding it nearly steady.

Warned by the noise of the hammer locking back, the swordswoman turned. Darla fired at pointblank range into the swordswoman's face. The powder in the flash pan burned in a sudden gray smoke wisp that curled toward the ceiling. The harsh crack of the pistol shot split the air even as fiery cinders spat from the barrel and burned into Moira's blouse.

The swordswoman fell backward and down, driven by the heavy pistol ball.

"This way!" Darla threw the pistol to the floor and grabbed Angelus by the hand.

Darius gazed at them from smoke-rimmed eyes. A crossbow quarrel protruded from one shoulder. "C'mon!"

Angelus bent down and removed a powder horn from the floor, left there by one of his men who had died or from a human who had left the tavern in a hurry. He grabbed the leather straps of two other powder horns in his other hand.

Darius sprinted for the tavern's fireplace. He stopped short, kicked a stained carpet from in front of the fireplace, and dug his fingers down into the wooden floor. When he lifted, a hatch opened. He dropped through, followed by another of his men who carried a lantern.

O'Domhnallain and his surviving men surged forward, spotting the escape route.

Angelus grabbed a table splattered with flaming oil and threw it into the warriors. They stumbled back, wreathed for a moment in the flames as their companions tried to help them extinguish the blaze. He dropped into the hole.

Angelus landed heavily on top of Darla. Getting to his feet, feeling the hard-packed ground beneath his boots, he pulled Darla after him. The scent of fresh-turned earth reminded him of the grave, and the air was thick, cloying.

The passageway was scarcely five feet wide and five feet high. The sides, top, and floor were uneven, carved by pick and shovel dozens of years in the past. Limestone pebbles and rocks gleamed in the weak light thrown out by the lantern.

Angelus ran as surefootedly as a cat. The lantern light ahead bobbed from side to side, throwing the passageway into momentary and uncertain relief. Angelus kept one hand running along the passageway's side.

Muffled thumps sounded behind.

Turning to take a quick look although he was certain he already knew what it was, Angelus saw one of O'Domhnallain's men standing in the tunnel under the escape hatch. The bull's-eye lantern the man held in one hand exploded light in Angelus's eyes.

"There they go!" someone cried out.

Angelus turned and redoubled his efforts to catch up with the others.

The tunnel direction curved and steadily went downward. The salt scent of the sea became stronger. Occasionally Angelus splashed through puddles that had seeped into depressions in the floor.

A few moments and perhaps two hundred yards farther down, the passageway opened into a large cave. The lantern light glimmered off the watery fingers the sea had thrust into the cave. Stalactites hung from the cavern overhead. Bats fluttered uncertainly, alerted by the swinging lantern.

"Go!" Angelus ordered. He'd already unscrewed the tops of the powder horns. Leaving two of the horns in a pile oozing gray-black gunpowder, he emptied most of the third powder horn over them, then poured a trail that led into the cave five feet.

Footsteps from the arriving warriors pounded down the hollow throat of the passageway.

Angelus took the lantern from his man, then smashed it across the end of the powder trail. The spilled flames licked at the powder trail hungrily, spitting sparks and fire, curling gray smoke above it. The powder burned slowly, but it moved deliberately back toward the waiting horns.

"Run!" Angelus shouted. Trailing the others, he ran, heading through the cold water ahead. The water plunged downward, the green waves tinted by the flickering light of the burning powder and the flaming oil. Soft sand lined the cave floor from years of erosion. Luckily, the water only got waist deep before Angelus was able to head up to land to the left near the mouth of the cave.

The hollow *boom!* of the exploding powder filled the cave with noise and flushed a gust of heated air out over Angelus. He turned, looking back in time to see a man get blasted from the passageway through the sudden cloud of powder smoke like a ball from a cannon's mouth.

The warrior had cinder patches sticking to him in places before he landed in the water and disappeared. He didn't come up again.

"Keep moving, damn ye!" Darius roared. "Them what that blast didn't kill won't be getting around any too soon, but the more distance we have betwixt us and them, the happier I'll be."

Angelus ran up the steep hillside, ears aching from the thunder that had slammed into them. Still, he laughed, exulting in the carnage he'd created. White foam curlers came in from the sea to splash across the narrow, pebbled shoreline below.

"Stay with the coastline, lad," Darius instructed. "That cave and passageway was an old smuggler's route that's still used now and again, but we're going to be better off being shut of this place. Mayhap they won't be after following us immediately, but I've got me a feeling they'll come."

Ignoring the pain that flared through his burns, Angelus ran. Whoever O'Domhnallain and his warriors were, Angelus had no doubts they would not give up too soon. They were too driven.

But the woman continued to haunt his thoughts as he ran across the hillside. He couldn't help wondering if Darla's pistol shot had killed the woman or if she'd been burned in the fire. He felt certain there was no way she could have escaped death yet again.

CHAPTER TEN

Angel woke in darkness, his thoughts still filled with Ireland nearly two hundred fifty years ago. In his mind he kept seeing the red-haired swordswoman falling back from Darla's pistol shot time after time. Moira's face remained cold and emotionless the whole time that she fell.

An uncontrolled shiver raced through Angel, and for a panicked moment he couldn't remember where he was. He peered through the darkness above him, sorting through all the memories.

When the past became too vivid, as it sometimes did because so much of his life had been filled with danger and violence, occasionally it was hard to remember where he was when he first woke. The office and home in L.A. were still too new to feel entirely comfortable or familiar.

Knowing sleep wasn't going to return easily, he

sat up on the couch in his living quarters. The rooms were quiet around him despite the fact that he knew it was well into morning outside.

"Are you all right?" Whitney stood in the open doorway to the bedroom. She wore one of Angel's shirts, which hung to mid-thigh on her. She'd bunched the sleeves up around her forearms.

"I'm fine." Angel sat on the couch wearing sweatpants. He checked the time on the clock on the wall and found it was only a little before nine A.M. These were not his normal sleeping hours, but he'd wanted to rest before the next day. Once he'd gotten her off to bed, he'd tried reading and had fallen asleep before he'd realized it.

"Bad dream?" Whitney asked.

"Yeah." Angel hesitated. *Bad dream, bad memory.* "Did I wake you?"

"Not really. I was already awake."

"Sorry."

"No problem. I just thought maybe I'd wake you if you didn't come out of it on your own."

That possibility presented some real problems. "Waking me isn't a good idea," Angel told her. "I don't usually sleep that deeply, and when I do it's better to leave me alone."

"You didn't seem to have any problems tonight."

"I guess not."

"Don't worry about it. I'm glad one of us is going to be rested."

"Can I get you something to drink?" Angel felt almost invaded with someone in his personal quarters. Doyle and Cordelia came down from time to time, but other than that he usually had the rooms to himself. *In this business, that'll probably change.* He got up and walked to the small refrigerator in the kitchen area.

"What have you got?" Whitney sat at the small dining room table in the center of the room.

Angel pushed the blood bags he drank from to the back of the refrigerator, covering them with a bag of salad. "Can I warm you up a glass of milk?" he asked. "Sometimes that helps a person sleep."

"Sure."

Angel retrieved the teakettle from the cabinet above the stove, put milk in it, turned on a burner, and waited.

He looked at Whitney. "It'll be just a minute till the milk heats."

Still amused, she nodded. "It usually is."

The lack of spontaneous conversation threw Angel off, but he figured if spontaneous conversation had come up, that would have thrown him off his stride as well.

"You have a lot of books," Whitney said, glancing at the shelves covering the walls.

"I like to read."

"What do you read?"

Angel shrugged. "Biographies. History. Philosophy. Occultism. Science."

"Wow, that's heavy reading. Why so many interests?"

"I don't know. I haven't really thought about it. I guess I just like thinking I can understand."

"Understand what?"

"Why."

"Because I want to get to know you a little better," Whitney answered.

Angel smiled. "No, that wasn't a question. *Why* is the answer to your question. I like to think maybe I can understand why people do what they do, something about their natures that makes them do it."

"Shrinks can give you the answer to that."

"Different shrink, different answer," Angel replied. "I keep hoping there's one big, cover-everything answer."

"Do you think there is?"

"No."

"Then why do you try to understand if you don't think you can?"

"Because I think it's important that I try."

"To understand others?"

Angel reflected for a moment, gathering his

thoughts. He hadn't had someone dig so deeply into him since Buffy, and remembering that was unsettling. He hadn't seen her since graduation day in Sunnydale when he'd helped destroy the mayor.

"If I understand others," he said finally, "I come closer to understanding myself. Understanding myself, where I fit in, is really important to me."

The tea kettle whistle blew and she jumped in her chair.

Angel poured the milk into the cup, then put the cup on the table and sat across from her.

"Aren't you having anything to drink?"

"I'm not the one having trouble sleeping."

"Right. That's why you were having that nightmare." Whitney blew on the milk and sipped cautiously. Her gray-green eyes, so direct like the others that Angel remembered, regarded him frankly. "Do you think you can do it?"

"What?" Angel noticed the challenging note in her voice.

"Keep me alive. Find out who's behind these attacks. Somehow manage to keep Gunnar's schedule for the show intact?"

"I don't know if I can do all of that," Angel said. "I'm going to start with keeping you alive and try to find out who is behind the attacks."

She sipped the milk again. "And if I choose to try to do the shoot today?"

"You've never been attacked on a set, so I think you should be safe there."

"And Gunnar will make sure all the security people stay in place."

Angel nodded.

Whitney sipped her milk again, not meeting his gaze.

Angel smelled the fear in her, and it bothered him. There were no guarantees even with his skills, strength, and knowledge that he could prevent someone from hurting her.

"It seems to me," she said, "that the smartest thing to do would be to hide out."

"If you did that, the people hunting you would have no reason to come forward. They'd hide out, too. Maybe they'd even go away for a while, waiting for you to put in another appearance. Even if you gave up this life, there's a chance they'd stay dedicated enough to find you."

Silence stretched between them.

"I don't want to give this up, Angel," she whispered. "God forgive me, but this is what I've been working toward all my life. It's not fair."

"No," Angel agreed. "It's not."

"But it would be easier to find these people if they were trying to find me?"

"Yes."

Whitney took a deep breath. "Then that's what

we'll do." She pushed herself up from the table. "I've got to get some sleep if I'm going to put in a full day's work."

Angel stood as well, realizing how fragile she looked in the dark room.

In the next moment she stepped into his arms. "Hold me for just a little while. It's been a long time since anyone just held me."

Hesitantly Angel put his arms around her. He felt her warm breath against his shoulder, sensed her pulse beating against the hollow in her throat. The dark hunger rose in him, sharp and demanding in the shadows that filled the room.

She held on to Angel with a quiet desperation.

"You're so cold," she whispered against his chest.

"I've . . . got a low blood temperature," he told her. "It's not dangerous, just different."

"I don't know how you stay warm." Her flesh seemed to sear his.

Angel didn't say anything. He just stood in the center of the room and held her.

"Ugh! Talk about the dead walking!" Cordelia glanced at her reflection in the hand mirror, then turned to Angel, who stood at her side but wasn't reflected. "Sorry. Talking about me, not you."

Angel gave a small nod. His attention was fixed

completely on Whitney across the street on the location shoot for *Dark Midnight*. The television crews had put up signs announcing that they were shooting, but he'd convinced Schend to pull them. There was no need to advertise where they were in case the people looking for Whitney didn't already know.

Cordelia put the mirror back in her purse. She'd dressed to draw attention that day. She wore dark gray Capri pants, topped off with a hot pink halter-style silk shantung shirt with an open back that showed off her tan.

The production crew formed a small island of humans and machinery on the other side of the street in front of Hannigan's, a bar that was featured in the *Dark Midnight* television series. Flint Boyd, the director, was spending time with Whitney and the other actors, laying out the scene for them.

Late-afternoon sunlight slanted across the rooftops, but the buildings were tall enough that only shadows actually touched the street. The marquee outside proclaimed: DARK MIDNIGHT CLOSED SET TONIGHT!

Cordelia knew the presence of the film crew that night would draw even more than the usual number of customers. A lot of television and movie acting hopefuls would put in an appearance, striving to get caught in the footage and be discovered. If things allowed that night, or she could convince Angel it might be in their best interests to know how the shoot later went, Cordelia knew she wanted to be there herself.

"So give," she told Angel.

"What?"

"Whitney spent the night at your place last night," Cordelia said. "As far as I know, that's the first film star you've ever spent the night with."

Angel didn't reply.

"I mean," Cordelia said with rising interest, "it was, wasn't it?"

Angel remained quiet, and for a moment Cordelia thought he wasn't going to answer. "Well," he said, "there was that whole Marilyn Monroe thing."

"You're kidding!"

"Yes," Angel said.

"Yes, you're kidding, or yes, it's true?"

"Kidding."

Cordelia quietly fumed. Despite the trust and friendship she had with Angel, there was so much she didn't know about him, about who he'd been with and where he'd been. A lot of it, she figured, was not her business, but probably even more of it was boring. *Or, during the wild blood-bingeing years, totally gross.*

"How did she do last night?" Cordelia asked. "Seeing your first dead body tends to leave an impression."

"She's scared," Angel replied.

Across the street Flint Boyd sent the actors and actresses to their marks, then followed them inside the bar himself. Two LAPD squad cars occupied either end of the street, keeping the crowd that had gathered there behind the red-and-white striped sawhorses.

"Believe it or not," Cordelia said, "I had that one figured."

"I've got a meeting at the sheriff's department to get to," Angel said. "Kate got me some time with the man they arrested. If you have any trouble, you should be able to reach me there."

"Do you think there's going to be any trouble?"

"No," Angel replied. "If I did, I wouldn't leave."

"Right. Because you know I'm not exactly Security Girl here."

"I know. I'll be back as soon as I can."

"Where's Doyle? I could use some backup here."

"Following up on the symbol. He'll be in touch, too. Until then just keep your eyes and ears open." Angel turned and walked away.

Sure, leave me with the potential target for a madman's bullet or knife. Cordelia remembered the man hanging from Whitney's ceiling. *Or hangman's noose. I can take it.*

Then she considered the options. Poking around in the off-the-beaten-path places Doyle was having to search in was in no way appealing. And if she wanted the whole *Silence of the Lambs* type of conversations women had with convicts in prison, she could log into a singles chat room and talk to the doofs that hung out there.

Across the street the *Dark Midnight* crew continued working, bringing the scene to life. Through the bar windows, Cordelia watched as the cast ran through their lines with the director watching. Gunnar Schend parked his Hummer beside the bar and went inside. According to the reports he'd given Whitney, who had in turn given them to Angel, the producer had been in meetings all day.

Cordelia moved closer to the crowd around the bar. Inside the bar Gunnar Schend took out his cell phone and started talking. He didn't look happy in no time flat. Whitney waved at him but didn't approach.

Schend angrily hung up the phone by folding it in on himself. Then he went to the bar and placed an order for what looked like a double.

Maybe the attacks on Whitney aren't the only problems he's having, Cordelia thought. She was used to looking for clues during her time as a Slayerette, and that definitely was a clue.

"Oh, my, my," someone behind Cordelia said. "And don't you just look stunning."

Suddenly on edge because a person couldn't tell for sure which way a comment like that was going to go, Cordelia spun and spotted the man behind her.

The man was at least six feet four inches tall and wore an electric blue Armani with an exact fit. His tousled hair held blond highlights and stood out against the dark tan that looked genuine and not fake-bake. His teeth were perfect and white.

"Who are you?" Cordelia asked.

The man produced a card seemingly from thin air with a flourish and a smile. "Davis Hollings."

The name clicked in Cordelia's mind instantly as she took the gold foil embossed card. Davis Hollings was the designer of NewNet, the latest search engine to hit the Internet with a big splash.

He also stalked Whitney and could have killed the security guard in Whitney's apartment last night.

"Who are you?" he asked.

"Cordelia Chase."

Hollings glanced toward the bar. "Are you in this scene?"

"Actually, no," Cordelia responded.

"You should be," Hollings said, sizing her up again. "You look like a great little actress to me. Are you in anything I know?"

"I'm kind of between jobs at the moment," Cordelia said.

"A young lady as pretty as you shouldn't be away from a camera lens for long. I stay pretty involved with television these days. Maybe I can hook you up with a producer or studio. I haven't found any out here who have a problem spending NewNet sponsor dollars."

Cordelia put the card in her purse. "Thanks."

Hollings cleared his throat. "Is Whitney around today?"

"In the bar." Cordelia saw his interest in her dwindle between drawn breaths. *Oh, man, he's like I'm-So-Much-In-Lust Guy.* She found it irritating. Back in Sunnydale she'd been among the elite every day of her life. Only her secret identity as Slayerette had pulled her into slumming with the commoners.

"I just wondered how she was holding up after last night," Hollings said.

"She's doing pretty well. It was really heavy into gruesome and horrifying."

Hollings glanced at her with renewed interest. "You were there?"

Now would be the time for one of those photo-

enhanced private investigator's license thingies.
Instead, Cordelia gave him a card.

" 'Angel Investigations,' " Hollings read. "I'd heard they were involved in the murder last night. You know them?"

"Actually," Cordelia said, "I'm one of them. A partner. A clue-gatherer type."

"What are you doing here today?"

"Watching over Whitney."

Hollings glanced at her with deliberate thoroughness that was supposed to be charming in a sleazy kind of way. "You don't seem to be carrying a pistol."

Cordelia crossed her arms and decided to dial up the vamp a notch. "It's concealed."

Hollings raised a flirting eyebrow. "Very well, may I add."

Cordelia smiled, knowing she had all his attention. "You may, and thank you." She paused, troubled a little as she caught up with everything he'd said. "You knew Angel Investigations was at Whitney's apartment last night? That wasn't in the news."

The media had splashed the television and radio broadcasts, newspapers and tabloids with the story all day long. So far there'd been no mention of Angel Investigations.

Detective Lockley had kept Angel out of the

news at Angel's request. Personally, Cordelia felt they could have used the exposure.

Hollings smiled again, but his eyes didn't hold amusement. "I make it my business to know what's going on with Whitney."

And that was the sound of a guy in total stalker mode. Cordelia kept her smile in place, but a cold wariness filled her.

"You sure dis be de place where you want to be stopping, mon?"

Doyle stared through the taxi's rear passenger side window. They were just north of South Central, and the neighborhood looked like a war zone.

Buildings had windows boarded over to prevent drive-by shootings or to keep from having to replace glass that was either broken or constantly a target for graffiti. The building fronts, including the plywood panels over the windows, still carried gang chops declaring territory as well as efforts by street artists looking to promote their own tags. Security bars covered the doors.

Most of the businesses appeared to be closed down, but hard-faced men and grim-faced youths sat on folding chairs around tables and racks that displayed merchandise they had to sell.

A small mom-and-pop grocery store on the corner had handmade paper signs plastered all over the plywood panels covering the windows. The signs fluttered in the afternoon's weak breeze. Only some of them had been replaced after being covered with graffiti.

But high on the right was a sign faded with age that hadn't been touched by spray paint at all. It simply read MAMA NTOMBI, and had an arrow pointing up.

If someone didn't know, Doyle guessed, *they'd think Mama Ntombi has a rooftop office instead of being located at the back of the grocery store.*

"Yeah," he said confidently. "This is the place."

The driver shook his head, making his dreadlocks quiver. "Mon, I tink you making big mistake. You don't mind my saying so, dis ain't no place for no whitebread like you."

"No," Doyle disagreed. "But there's a Chinese laundry I can think of that makes this place look like home."

The driver grinned, flashing gold teeth in the rearview mirror. "Mon, you in hock with Yuan?"

"You know Yuan?"

"Did Yuan show you his collection yet, mon?"

"What collection?"

The driver laughed. "His toes, mon. Ol' Yuan is into toes big-time. Say someone don't pay up on time, dey gotta give up a toe. Kind of an extra down payment on de money a fella owes."

"You're kidding." Doyle felt almost nauseated even after everything he'd seen before Angel and since. Monsters and demons and such were one thing, but people acting like them was just wrong.

"No, mon." The driver shook his head. "I'm deadly serious about dis ting." He slipped off a shoe and raised his leg. His right foot had only four toes, a bright pink and white scar showing where his little toe had been. "Me, I don't place no more bets at dat place. Mon go in dere, tinking he's gonna be getting a foot in de door toward a sure ting? He better count his toes coming back out, dat's all I'm saying."

Doyle really didn't want to know, but he couldn't help asking. "What does Yuan do with the toes?"

"Mon, he keeps dem in dese jars. Shakes 'em up now and again, den watches dem fall to de bottom like one of dem snow globes. And he just laughs like it someting he *never* seen before."

Doyle pushed the money into the pass-through tray mounted in the front seat. "Keep the change."

"Sure, mon, and I tank you." The driver counted the bills with an experienced thumb flick. "Maybe you want me to wait around for you, mon. If dis business of yours be pretty quick."

Looking at the harsh appearance of the neighborhood, Doyle nodded. "You know, I think maybe that's a good idea."

"You tink maybe you leave me an advance, mon?"

Doyle peeled a ten off and put it into the tray. Then he opened the door and stepped out onto the curb. He was conscious of the fact that he drew attention immediately. The security-bar-covered door was heavy and hard to move, dragging across the rubber WELCOME mat that had been permanently scarred with scuff marks and gum.

An old black man with wiry gray hair around his bald spot and skinny arms stacked canned food in a cardboard box for a little old woman and the sullen teenager beside her. "Can I help you?" the man asked.

"I'm looking for Mama Ntombi," Doyle replied.

"Straight back past the meat lockers and bathrooms. The men's is out. You want to go, you got to use the ladies'."

Doyle waved and made his way across the concrete floor through the aisles of canned goods and potato chips. He ducked the hanging scales by the vegetable bins and kept going.

Mama Ntombi's office was tucked away in a small room between metal stock shelves that leaned threateningly. Doyle almost had to turn sideways to get through. Beaded strings woven of white plastic skulls and black and red stones served as a door. Incense smoke drifted out in blue-gray waves. The scent was heady and cloying, drawing a series of coughs and sneezes from Doyle as he stood outside.

"Come in, boy," a hoarse voice ordered.

Doyle parted the bead strings and stepped into a small, dark room. The incense smoke pooled against the ceiling, further dimming the candle-light in the room.

A shriveled old black woman sat on the other side of the small secretary's desk that nearly filled the room. She wore a plum-colored dress that had a lot of embroidered symbols in neon-bright strings. The symbols included silver moons, golden stars, ivory skeletons, and lime-green birds.

"Sit." Mama Ntombi gestured to a straight-backed pink and purple chair that looked as if it had been liberated from a fast-food restaurant. Three lighted candles in the shape of skeletons posed in suggestive positions provided the only illumination.

Doyle sat and looked into the yellowed eyes. "You're Mama Ntombi?"

"That I be, boy, for all these years and more." The old woman's pink gums showed, her lips wrinkled and caved in around them. She lifted a pipe from an overflowing ashtray at her side, tamped it a couple times with a disposable lighter, and lit up. "You come here with a problem lying heavy on your heart."

In the circles Doyle traveled in the city while helping Angel, Mama Ntombi wasn't just a fakir hustling rent money. She was reputed to be truly connected to the Voudoun gods. She had come from Haiti originally, and some people Doyle had talked to had said that was one hundred and fifty years ago.

She took another puff on the pipe, let the smoke wreathe her head. "You got a gift for seeing, too, don't you, boy?" She took Doyle's hand before he could pull away. Her flesh felt leathery, dry and desiccated, like it was freshly unwrapped from the tomb. "You don't have control of your gift, though."

"No." Doyle looked into those old eyes, thinking they could see right through him.

"Pity. It's a strong one. A man could live on the power you have if you learned to channel it properly. But it's not yours to learn and control, is it?"

Doyle was surprised at her insight, and he believed in her enough that it scared him. "Maybe, but that's not why I'm here."

"No," Mama Ntombi told him, "you're here about the woman. The one with the red-gold hair."

*　　*　　*

"Are you Angel?"

"Yeah." Angel looked at the sheriff's deputy seated on the other side of the desk in the small office. He felt nervous inside the sheriff's office.

"Got any ID?"

"No."

The deputy looked up at him, eyes narrowing suspiciously. He was tall and lean, whipcord and rawbone, with a Colt Government Model .45 on his hip. The uniform was clean and pressed, and the nametag on his left breast gave his name as Pearson. "Letting someone in without the proper ID isn't going to happen."

"Kate Lockley said you'd be able to help me."

"She said I'd be helping a guy named Angel."

"That's me."

"I asked her if that was a first name or a last name. She said she didn't know."

Angel didn't say anything.

"Maybe Kate knows you," Pearson said, "but I don't."

"That's why I showed up."

Angel glanced over his shoulder and found Kate Lockley standing there. She wore khaki pants and a yellow shirt under a brown blazer. Her blond hair was pulled back in a ponytail.

"You send me a guy without ID and I'm supposed to run him through the jail?" Pearson complained.

"I'm his ID," Kate replied.

The sheriff's deputy glanced at Angel again. "Do you know how far you're sticking your neck out? How far you're asking me to stick my neck out?"

"You owe me," Lockley stated clearly.

Pearson stared back at her, and Angel knew that whatever debt existed between the two wasn't a friendly one. After a moment, Pearson broke the eye contact and opened the desk drawer in front of him. He made out two ID badges.

"You got a favorite first name, Angel?" the deputy asked.

"No."

"Fine, then I'll pick one. Even rock stars don't get in here with only one name." Pearson pushed the ID tags to the other side of the desk and looked up at Kate. "You know the way. I'll call ahead."

Kate took the IDs and handed one over to Angel. She left the office without another word. "He'll remember you," she warned.

"I had that feeling." Following Kate's lead, Angel pinned the ID badge to his shirt.

They walked down the corridor and passed through two checkpoints. Kate had to surrender her weapon at the first one. An overweight deputy checked them off on the clipboard he held.

"You're here to see the John Doe from the truck stop last night?" the deputy asked.

"Yes," Kate replied. "Has he been Mirandized?"

"If he speaks English, Korean, Japanese, Spanish, or Ebonics, he has," the deputy replied, pushing the button that opened the last security door. "But since he hasn't spoken since we brought him in, we don't know."

"He speaks English," Angel said. "He threatened Whitney Tyler last night."

"Amazingly," the deputy said, "that doesn't count in the court's eyes. A good attorney will argue that this mook was only saying what someone taught him to say, without knowing what it meant."

"He attacked Whitney Tyler," Angel pointed out.

"Oh, he can be tried on his actions, but the district attorney still has to prove he can understand what he's on trial for. They do wrong, but we're the ones gotta do it right. Go figure."

Kate followed the trustee through the checkpoint, and the heavy steel door clanged shut behind them. Angel felt a brief surge of claustrophobia but quickly pushed it out of his mind.

"You okay?" Kate asked.

"That door shutting was a little too absolute for me," Angel admitted.

"Don't worry," Kate said with a smile, tapping her ID badge, "we've got Get Out of Jail Free cards." She glanced at his. "Johnny Angel, huh? Pearson's got a sense of humor."

"I guess you'd have to know him to see it."

Kate chuckled and walked by the long rows of cells. Prisoners got up from their bunks and started calling out obscene suggestions. She kept walking and ignored them.

The coarse vulgarity offended Angel, and he felt the back of his neck tightening and reddening. The dark hunger that twisted in his guts constantly rose up threateningly in reaction to the threats, pulling at his features.

"Don't," Kate said.

"What?" Angel touched his face, wondering if she'd seen something there.

"Don't respond to them," she said.

"It's hard to ignore."

"You don't get used to it," Kate admitted, "but you do get to where you can tune it out." She smiled ruefully. "To tell you the truth, after I have to visit here or the city jail, I usually have to take a shower as soon as I can to feel clean again." She stopped at a cell on the left.

Angel peered through the bars.

Even sitting down on crossed legs between the bed chained to the wall and the stainless steel toilet, the man looked tall. He wore an orange jumpsuit, his back straight and his face blank of emotion. His left leg was in a bright, white cast from the knee down. If he saw them there, he gave no indication. His lower lip was swollen, congealed blood sitting on it. His head was bruised in several places, and one eye was purpled and nearly swollen shut.

"Can I get in to see him?" Angel asked.

The trustee was a big man, shaved bald with a gunslinger mustache. Gray scars tracked his black skin. He glanced at Kate. "I don't know if that's such a good idea. This guy got loose this morning after we took him back from the infirmary. Took six guys to put him back in his cage, and him with a broke leg. He sent two deputies to the hospital."

Kate looked at Angel. "The deal was talk to him, not visit."

"Standing out here isn't going to work," Angel said.

Kate hesitated only a moment. "Open the door."

Reluctantly the trustee opened the heavy door and rolled it back. The prisoner didn't even seem to take notice.

Angel moved cautiously inside the cell. He could smell the scent of Galway Bay inside the small room, and its presence was shocking. He breathed in again but smelled only the disinfectants used to keep the cell clean.

The man stood, uncoiling in the liquid movement of a trained athlete despite the cast.

Angel spoke, keeping his voice light, "I'm—"

"I know what you are," the man whispered hoarsely. Evidently he'd been hit in the throat as well.

Angel studied the man's face. "I don't know you."

"No."

"Why are you after Whitney Tyler?"

"I follow the trail of a hellbeast," the man said softly. "I have staked my honor and my life, that I may follow the divine path I have been led to."

"Whitney Tyler is a hellbeast," Angel said. He was vaguely aware that he had Kate's and the trustee's attention, but he hoped that they thought he was playing along with the man, getting him to talk.

The man looked at him. "You don't know, do you?"

"Know what? I don't understand what you're talking about."

"All these years you've been walking this earth, yet you bother to learn so little."

"Tell me about Whitney Tyler."

"There is no Whitney Tyler. She is an abomination just as you are an abomination."

Without warning the man drove a fist into Angel's face. Angel's head snapped back, rattling off the bars behind him. The man had hit harder than anything human. Before Angel could recover, the man was on him, gripping his head in both hands. He was aware that Kate and the trustee were trying to get the cell door open.

The man's bruised and battered face filled Angel's vision. His spittle flecked Angel's cheek as he strained and started twisting Angel's head. "If I twist your head off, will you die?"

CHAPTER ELEVEN

As the old woman held Doyle's hand, a sudden surge of pain rattled his brain, starting at his shoulders and seeming to shoot through his skull. A vision descended over him, strong enough and different enough that he knew it wasn't caused from the abilities the Powers That Be gave him, taking him back to the ship in the middle of the wild, bucking ocean. He wanted to scream at the old woman to get out of his mind, but he didn't have the strength.

"Let me use my power," the old woman said. "I can show you what I see."

Moonlight silvered the blades that danced in the hands of Angelus and the woman warrior with red-gold hair. Again, Doyle was acutely aware of the woman's resemblance to Whitney Tyler. He returned to the present, staring into Mama Ntombi's rheumy yellow eyes.

Mama Ntombi sat leaning back in her chair, puffing on her pipe with consternation. "This thing you be chasing, boy, it's old and it's powerful. Ain't no thing to be triflin' with if you got a choice."

"I don't have a choice." Doyle reached into his pocket. "How much for your help?"

"I can't help you that much," she replied. "All I know is that I can point you in a direction. What you find out from there is up to you."

"Fair enough." In the past Doyle had learned that information in those secret circles was often as hard to interpret or come by as his visions. Mysterious ways were basically mysterious by definition.

"It gonna cost you one hundred dollars for my time, boy."

Doyle counted the money out and passed it over. Normally he might have haggled, but not after seeing the demonstration she'd just given.

"What you have for me?" the old woman asked.

Doyle unfolded the paper napkin Angel had drawn on the night before. He'd stopped and made copies at a Kinko's, but he didn't want to show the old woman one of those. He wanted her in touch with the original to give her skills a better chance to work.

Mama Ntombi smoothed the folds from the napkin, seeming mesmerized by the lines. "The one who drew this, boy, he has him a strong hand."

"Yes," Doyle agreed.

"And he carries much pain within him, old and new."

"Do you know what this symbol is?" Doyle asked. He was uncomfortable with how much the old woman seemed able to read into the drawing.

"This ain't no voodoo symbol."

"No, but voodoo has its roots in Christianity and Catholicism. Is this something bastardized from one of those?"

Mama Ntombi nodded. "You right about that. But you holding something back." Despite being as elderly as she was, she reached across the table too quickly for him to move.

When her fingertips rested against the back of his hand, another vision slammed into Doyle's mind, shoved into place by the incredible power the old woman possessed. He was back in Whitney's apartment staring at the harsh words written on the walls. He focused on PURGATORY. The room returned around him when she drew her hand away.

"Purgatory," Mama Ntombi repeated. "That is from the Catholic belief, the place trapped between heaven and hell."

"Yeah." Doyle took his hands from the table and leaned back in his chair.

She smoothed the paper napkin on the tabletop. "You have come to the right place, boy. I recognize this symbol."

The muscles in Angel's neck quivered and felt as if they were tearing loose from the incredible strain they were under. His attacker kept twisting his head. Vertebrae popped, close to the breaking point.

"Open the damn door!" Kate reached through the bars and grabbed the prisoner's face as she yelled at the trustee. She locked her fingers around the prisoner's cheek and gouged at his eye.

Angel heard the trustee yanking on the door, but the combined weight of himself and the prisoner were preventing it from unlocking. Black spots swam in Angel's vision, swelling to fill all his sight. He clasped his hands together, then drove them upward, smashing through the prisoner's hold.

The prisoner's grip broke, but he immediately tried to get hold again.

Pain shot through Angel's neck and across his shoulders as he rocked on his feet. The prisoner came at him without pause, launching a flying kick. Angel dodged to the side, sweeping his left arm out to push the man's feet farther away.

The prisoner's bare feet collided with the bars, nearly trapping Kate's arm. She pulled back, yanking her arm out of the cell. Even as his forward momentum came to a sudden stop, the prisoner dropped and rolled back, getting to his feet easily. He came for Angel, arms outstretched.

Angel blocked the searching hands against his left forearm, then drove the other hand into the prisoner's stomach twice. He stepped in, but his attacker lashed out with splayed fingers, seeking his eyes. Dodging back, Angel managed to get just out of the man's reach. The cell was eight feet long, leaving either of them hardly any room to move.

The prisoner feinted with his hands, then when Angel stepped in to go on the attack again, he drove an elbow into Angel's forehead. Driven backward, Angel slammed against the bars behind him. The prisoner was on him before he could recover.

The dark hunger swirled within Angel, urging him to go to full vamp-face and use all the strength and ferocity at his command in order to survive. The man's hands circled his head again, covering his temples and ears, locking around the back of his head.

"Now you will seek the true death, fiend," the man snarled. Blood ran from the corner of one of his eyes. "There will be no more easy life for you." He twisted with the inexorable pressure again.

Angel slammed his open palm straight up, catching his attacker on the chin hard enough to daze him. As the man stumbled back, Angel caught him with a roundhouse kick that hammered him back against the bars.

The prisoners in the other cells cheered, drawn by the prospect of blood and violence. Two more uniformed deputies rushed down the hallway between the cells.

Angel snap-kicked the man in the face, finding the rhythm for his moves even in the small cell now. The man reached for him, but Angel slapped the arm away and followed up with another roundhouse kick that caught the man in the stomach and drove the breath from him.

The prisoner dropped to his knees, one ankle stiffly encased in the cast, but his eyes stayed locked on Angel, hatred and fervor brimming in them.

Angel locked his fingers in the man's sweat-streaked hair and gripped tightly. Then he caught one of the prisoner's arms and pulled it around behind the man, lifting it high on his shoulder to immobilize him. Angel yanked the man's head back, putting his face close.

"Why are your people after Whitney Tyler?" he demanded.

"I told you," the man croaked.

"They went to her place last night," Angel said, "and they killed the security guard on duty there."

The man's eyes never lost their conviction. "No. My brothers would never do that."

"They did."

The prisoner's voice thickened. "No. We are sworn. Sworn to protect lives. We destroy demons; we are not life-takers like you. Our missions are sanctioned by our deity, made clear by the training we are provided, made holy by our prayers."

"You drove a truck through the wall of a diner," Angel went on. "You could have killed people yesterday yourself."

Kate and the deputy struggled with the cell door.

"But I didn't."

Angel shook his head. "You couldn't know that."

"There are things in this world and in others that a mortal and even immortal mind cannot know," the man responded.

Angel saw the conviction in the madman's gaze. *He believes what he's saying.*

"You know what I'm telling you is true," the man said. "Just as I tell you that I believed no one would be killed last night, I'm also telling you that none of my brothers would kill that guard. Look elsewhere for your answer to that riddle. Look elsewhere and I promise you'll find the trail that had been laid."

"What will it take to make them leave Whitney alone?"

"They cannot break from their task. We have searched for her before, but she has been clever."

"If she was so clever, how did she get caught now?"

"There is a spark of good that yet lingers in her. She doesn't know what she is."

"What is she?" Angel demanded.

All the fight left the man as the trustee finally got the cell door open. He charged across the room and grabbed the prisoner's other arm, slamming his face against the cell bars.

"She's your death come walking," the man promised hoarsely, trying to hold Angel's gaze even as the trustee slapped a pair of cuffs on him, locking his hands behind his back. "You can't trust her."

The conviction in the man's words rested uneasily in Angel's mind. One of the arriving deputies grabbed him by the shoulders and shoved him toward the open cell door.

"Out!" the deputy commanded.

Kate took Angel's arm and pulled him from the

cell. Angel watched as the deputies bound the prisoner's legs with cuffs as well.

"We're going to have to get a doctor in here to check on him," the trustee said. The man was clearly not happy. He scanned Angel. "Are you okay? He looked like he busted you up pretty good."

"I'm fine," Angel replied.

"Then I suggest you get the hell out of here," the trustee said. "You've done enough here."

"C'mon," Kate said, pulling Angel away. "We've got to talk."

Angel walked at her side as they headed back to the checkpoint, wondering what he was going to tell the detective.

Doyle looked at the old woman across the napkin with the symbol on it. "What is it?"

"It is a thing that belongs to a group who once belonged to the Catholics before finding their own beliefs. They called themselves the Blood Cadre." Mama Ntombi sucked on her pipe again as she pushed the napkin back across the table. "Have you heard of the Jesuit order?"

Doyle nodded. "Kind of a warrior for God. Rode out and smote down unbelievers, did conversions whether the guy they were talking to wanted to be converted or not. Built schools, swore vows of poverty but made sure plenty of gold made its way into the coffers of the Church. Started by Saint Ignatius Loyola."

"Yes. Them men and women of the Jesuits, they were very strong in their beliefs, very unforgiving in their defense of them. They are hard, driven hunters who deliver the wrath of their god more than tender mercies. The Blood Cadre was another group of them, a splinter group that completely separated from the parent organization. They chose to stand against the undead and demons, and they worked in the shadows between good and evil. Evil things fought them, hunted them when they thought they could take them. And even the original Jesuits shunned them because they were so violent. You don't be careful in this world, boy, you end up becoming like them what you hunt."

Doyle pulled at his T-shirt collar with a forefinger. "Took things kind of personally, did they?"

"Those creatures who lived by night and those who chose to walk in darkness learned to fear the Blood Cadre."

"They're still around?"

"The paper you have in your hand says this is so. I know they still walked the lands in secrecy a hundred years ago when I was a little girl."

"Where did you see them?"

"In Berlin. It was in the eighteen nineties. I was a young girl and had not even seen my sixteenth birthday."

Doyle did the math on that one, realizing that Mama Ntombi claimed to be nearly one hundred and twenty years old. *That's old for a human,* he thought, *but that's only half Angel's age.* He pushed that out of his mind.

"I was there with my poppa," the old woman said. "He took him a trip to Germany to see about some business. And it was there in Germany that I met this man, this warrior of the Blood Cadre." She smiled at the memory. "Ah, and he was a fine warrior, too. Tall and strong, with blond hair and piercing blue eyes. Just looking at him made my heart beat faster. I was so young and so inexperienced, I fell in love with him. He came, pretending to be a man on business. Two nights later I saw him kill one of them German men we were staying with who was a werewolf."

"How do you know he was a member of the Blood Cadre?" Doyle asked.

"Killing that werewolf wasn't no easy thing," the old woman answered. "Killing any shapeshifter requires skill and daring and luck. The warrior had most of those things, but he was hurt. He left him a blood trail behind and I followed it. I found him the next day in a cave in the forest, him burning up from a fever and out of his head. I used my knowledge of herbs and such to fix a poultice and give him something to bring the fever down."

"He told you he was part of the Blood Cadre?"

"No, boy, but he had him a fierce fever. The kind that drives men to talking and to living in their fears and their past while they suffer through it. He talked a lot during his fever periods because they came and went. Even with everything I did and him being a strong man like he was, I thought for a while I was going to lose him."

Doyle listened, mesmerized by the story, wondering how it was going to tie into what he was looking for.

"Couldn't seem to shut him up some days and just knew him raving was going to alert some of them Germans. It was one of them times that he told me he was a member of the Blood Cadre. And I saw the silver ring he wore. That ring had this symbol on it, and he said it was how other warriors knew each other, that sometimes they were even kept secret from each other so those who journey from their keeps would be more safe."

Doyle glanced back at the napkin drawing, finding it even more intriguing now.

"You've seen the ring before, boy." Mama Ntombi stared straight at him.

"I think I'd remember seeing it if I did."

The old woman held her hand out. "Let me show you."

Reluctantly, dreading the coming experience, Doyle put his hand in hers, then felt her power take hold of him. Immediately the memory stirred in his mind, bringing up the image of the woman warrior standing on a ship's deck.

And there in the moonlight, a silver band gleamed on the woman warrior's hand. This time the vision was clear enough that Doyle could see that the ring bore the symbol.

"Did any of what that man said to you make any sense?"

Angel looked at Kate Lockley. "No." And he felt a little better because most of that answer was true.

They stood in the visitors' waiting room. Chairs and vending machines lined the walls. A handful of people sat in the chairs, and none of them looked happy. A young mother with two small children clinging quietly to her knees looked as if she'd been crying.

"Why did he talk to you?" she asked. "He's not even talked to anyone else here."

"I don't know. Maybe it's because I'm actually working for Whitney, trying to protect her."

"How does he know that? He was picked up before you took on the case."

"I don't know."

"Is there something I'm missing?"

"Kate," Angel said gently, "you brought me into this, remember? I had no idea these people even existed until they showed up in my office."

"Maybe that was a mistake."

Angel shrugged. "I think Schend told me you advised him that I had a way with offbeat cases."

"Yes. But this one has taken a different spin. I have to wonder if that was because you are now involved."

"The security guard was killed in Whitney's apartment while Schend hired me." Angel glanced at the two children clinging to the young mother's knees. The sadness in their eyes touched him deeply. There were some things that couldn't be avoided no matter what. He had that feeling of premonition now.

"This thing with Whitney Tyler is going to be a train wreck," Kate said softly.

"Maybe."

"You could step away from it."

"Sure."

"But you're not going to."

Angel met Kate's gaze. "No." He couldn't explain to her that walking away wasn't an option. He'd relocated to L.A. to get a chance to start over, to do something with his life.

He'd gone out into the morning months ago, expecting the sun to rise and burn him down, willing to let go of the unlife that remained to him because he just couldn't believe in anything else again. Then an unexpected snowstorm in Sunnydale had obscured and delayed the dawn, letting him see that something else lay ahead of him. For a time afterward he hadn't known what that path was, but he had found it, and now he was sure of it.

"Then there are a few things you should know," Kate told him. "Gunnar Schend may not be as protective of Whitney Tyler as he appears to be. The guy's heavy into gambling, but he's locked into the high rollers. Vice took down a bookie operation in Beverly Hills last week and found Schend's name on the computer files."

"Schend's in deep?"

"They don't keep the winners on those lists, Angel."

"How deep?"

"Over a million dollars."

Angel considered the information. "They gave him that kind of credit?"

Kate shrugged. "He's the producer of a hit television series at a time when those are about as rare as dinosaurs."

"Can he come up with the money?"

"Not and live his life in the style to which he's become accustomed. There are people who are looking for him, and he's managed to buy himself a little time, but not much. And he's the type to be convinced that he can break even on the next roll of dice."

Angel thought briefly of the television producer. Schend was the kind to live off the excitement of winning and losing, a natural born gambler who craved the adrenaline.

"After the first attacks on Whitney," Kate went on, "the detectives in the sheriff's office poked around and discovered that Schend had an insurance policy on Whitney Tyler for a couple million dollars."

"Is that unusual?" Angel asked.

"Not really. Actors and actresses are insurance-poor sometimes. Some studios pay for the policies. But Schend has a life insurance policy on Whitney."

"When did he take it out?"

"About halfway through the season."

"When did the heavy gambling start?"

"About halfway through the season. You can do the math on this one."

"Still might not mean anything."

"True, but I thought you'd want to know you might need to guard your back."

"I appreciate that." Angel shifted, suddenly anxious to get back to Whitney. Instead of alleviating some of the mystery about the attacks on the woman, the visit to the jail had only twisted it more deeply.

"Did you drive out?" Kate asked.

Angel shook his head.

"Do you have a way back into the city?"

"I planned on calling a cab." Angel knew from the clock on the wall and the darkness outside that dusk had come.

"I can save you cab fare if you're interested," Kate offered.

"You see, I was telling you the truth about them rings."

Doyle felt the vision ebbing from his grasp, trying desperately to hang on to it and squeeze some sort of understanding from it. *Why does that woman look so much like Whitney Tyler?* He had no clue.

"That vision is one from a long time ago," he told Mama Ntombi, finally certain of that. It wasn't Whitney in some kind of period piece. "What does that have to do with now?"

The old woman sucked on her pipe and spewed another cloud of smoke into the air. "I can see the vision as clearly as you, boy, but I can't be reading too much into it. But I know the answer is there."

"What?"

"A great evil, boy. A great evil done and a great evil coming. You know yourself that true evil can't be avoided. Sure, a man or a woman, they can delay it for a time, spend their lives running. But they ain't no place far enough away they can run to and make evil go away. For evil to make its peace, it's got to be faced up to, and a blood price paid. And that man you be friends with has got it to do."

Doyle felt like a small child again, caught doing something he knew he shouldn't have been doing. "Why Angel?"

"Any man who has known evil up close and personal," Mama Ntombi said, "stood up and welcomed evil into his home and his heart, he's a man ain't never going to know a day without thinking about evil. Evil's like an old ghost what can't be chased away even by the most powerful magics. I seen some in my time." She cackled with glee. "Hell, I probably be one I ever decide to give up the flesh. Got people I know I'd like to go to they house and rattle chains all night."

Doyle's skin crawled because he knew she was speaking the truth. He had his own evils he had yet to face before he could make any kind of peace with himself. That was one of the reasons he'd been brought to Angel.

"You friend in that vision," Mama Ntombi went on, "he close to that evil in some way. Some old debt come back to haunt him."

"He's changed," Doyle said desperately.

"Maybe he be okay then," the old woman suggested. "If he's got enough strength to do what he needs to do, maybe he'll be all right. But I know this walk going to be long and hard."

Doyle took the money from his pocket, letting the old woman see it. "You said sometimes you could see the future."

"Yes, the gods willing."

"How much would you charge me to tell me about the future of this?" Even if it ran him short on the money he owed Yuan, Doyle wasn't going to let Angel walk into danger if there was a way to see his friend clear.

"Put your money away, boy," Mama Ntombi snapped. "I done told you everything I could. Maybe more than I should. I don't sit back here in this little room to fleece tourists." She smiled. "Well, at least not all the time. Got to make my rent somehow. But you walk in some of the same circles where I go, so I tell it to you like it is."

Doyle put the money away.

"Listen to Mama Ntombi, boy. You and your

friend, you learn all you can about this evil. Knowing an evil, recognizing it, admitting it's there, that takes away some of that evil's strength. Don't make it go away, don't keep it from carving your skull clean some night and drinking down your soul, but maybe it levels the battlefield a little."

Mind spinning with all the implications in her words and the knowledge she'd give him, Doyle stood. He put an extra fifty dollars on the table without a word.

"There is something else you should do, boy."

Doyle looked at the old woman.

"You owe a man a debt."

Caught off guard, Doyle smiled wryly. "You get your dry-cleaning done at Yuan's or something?"

Mama Ntombi grinned, flashing pink gums. "I picked that up out of your thoughts, but it's not my business. What I do know, though, is that if you go make arrangements about this debt, your path will cross that of another, someone who will help you have a clearer understanding of what it is you face."

"What?"

"That's not for me to say."

Doyle considered that quickly. "Did you happen to see anything about toes?" he asked as nonchalantly as he could. "Because I've gotten kind of used to being able to fill out a sock, you know."

"I say a prayer for you tonight, boy. And one for your friend."

Angel rode the elevator down to the sheriff's office parking area with Kate. It took him a moment to realize she was talking to him.

Kate gave him a half-smile. "You're obviously not on this planet, so either John Doe shorted your brain more than you're admitting or you're obsessing on something."

"Just trying to make sense of why these people would be after Whitney."

"It's this town," Kate said. "Glamour. Glitz. And the eternal race for stardom. It's enough to make most people crazy."

"You're not."

"I'm in law enforcement. That's enough to make people wonder. And you don't know me well enough to make that judgment."

In spite of the situation, Angel smiled. "Maybe you're right."

"So what are you thinking? We're not talking about a group of loosely connected attacks anymore. And the security guard's death makes it a homicide now. The detectives working that case are going to want to talk to Whitney more closely now."

"Makes sense."

"By staying with Whitney and not knowing who these people are, you're also a target."

"I know."

"What I'm getting at is that you don't know your client. The homicide team is going to dig into her background, and they're going to look more closely than any media team ever has."

"And what do you expect them to find?" Angel asked.

"I don't know, but I'm thinking there's something. Guys like that nutcase in that cell upstairs don't just crawl out of the woodwork for no reason."

Angel was quiet a moment as they walked across the parking area. He heard an engine start up, the gentle roar contained in the building, but he ignored it. "She's an innocent, Kate." Even if he wasn't sure exactly what Whitney was, he was convinced of that. At least, partially innocent. Images of the warrior woman he'd fought all those years ago in Galway danced in his head. She'd been an innocent, too.

"What makes you so sure?"

Angel looked at her. "I know innocence when I see it. I've seen plenty that wasn't."

"The homicide guys are going to be brutally thorough," Kate said. "That may be something else she—and you—aren't used to."

"I've been around policemen a lot," Angel replied. "I know how they can be."

Kate stopped at the driver's side of her car and took her keys from her jacket pocket. "If you need anything," she said, "I can't guarantee that I can help you."

Angel started to say that he understood, but he saw the man step from behind a nearby maroon van and nod to him.

The man was tall and narrow, maybe twenty pounds too light for his frame. He wore a long, shiny black leather coat, a black shirt, and black pants. His black shoes held a high gloss. Short gray hair stood straight up, mirroring the close-cropped beard that covered his sunken cheeks. His eyes were glacial gray.

He lifted his coat and pointed to the pistol at his belt. Then he nodded at Kate, who hadn't seen him.

"Uh, give me just a minute," Angel said. "There's a guy I need to talk to."

Kate crawled in behind the steering wheel. She looked at the man, but his coat again concealed the pistol. "Friend of yours?"

"Not exactly. If you're in a hurry, I can take a cab." And if she left, Kate wouldn't be there for the man to menace.

"I don't mind waiting."

Angel nodded and strode over to the man, putting himself in between Kate and a clear shot, blocking the view of each from the other.

The gleam of silver on the man's gloved hand drew Angel's attention. Even at the distance he recognized the symbol the ring bore, knew it matched the one that had been found in Whitney's apartment.

And he remembered about the rings.

CHAPTER TWELVE

North of Clifden, Ireland

"Did you see them rings they wore? Did you see them rings the hellions wore back there?" Darius asked. "I'd bet you could get a good price for just one of them."

Huddled against a tree in the dark forest they'd run to in hopes of escaping the men who chased them, Angelus shook his head. The cave mouth they'd fled from after escaping the attack at the tavern lay two days back. But their pursuers were scarcely a half hour away, hindered by the night that surrounded them.

The warriors had regrouped in Clifden and had tracked them within just hours. For part of the first day, they'd traveled to a logging camp to the north of the city and high in the verdant green hills. But they'd not gotten to rest there long. Aside from being ferocious warriors, the men were also good hunters, managing to find their trail through streams and across rocky, broken land.

Angelus stared at the stream that ran bright and quick between the tall mountains around them. It reflected the harsh burn of the full moon's light. The burbling sound it made as it rushed over the rocks between the banks filled the narrow valley between the high mountains. The slight spray of the water smashing up against the banks was cold and quickly dampened his clothes. "Maybe you should stay here and take them."

"Damn me," Darius cursed as he looked at the white-capped water. "I ain't no fool, and fording that stream between these mountains is going to take us longer than I thought." He followed the course of it with his eyes. "If we had a good long-boat, we could be to sea afore them witchfinders could know where we'd gone."

The stream flowed up over the narrow banks in places, whitecaps coiling briefly around boulders and washing across their chosen trail. Fifty yards farther on, the stream twisted around a curve of the passage to the right and vanished from sight. There was no way to tell how much farther it ran.

"We're wasting time," Angelus stated. "Lead us on or get the hell out of the way."

Darius started to say something, but they were all aware of the riders visible behind them now.

Angelus glared at the bent grass they'd left behind them. Nearly as tall as a man, their passage could have been seen even by human vision. Another half-hour or hour at most and the grass would have sprung back up.

But their lead was no longer that big. Once the trail had started heading straight for the valley, the warriors had turned and started directly for it, no longer fanning out to make sure they missed nothing in their pursuit.

Darius ordered one of the men to take the lead along the narrow bank of the stream, and they proceeded in single file.

Glancing at the white-capped water, Angelus guessed that the stream might be as much as three or four feet deep in most places, perhaps as much as six or eight feet in the deepest part of the channel. But the force of the rushing stream would have slowed them tremendously if they'd tried to fight it.

Angelus followed Darla, watching to see where she stepped. She fell behind the captain and the pirates. At first Angelus thought it was because she couldn't maintain the pace, something he'd never witnessed before. He grew concerned and tried to help her.

Behind them, the mounted warriors steadily closed the distance, shearing away minutes.

"We're falling behind," Angelus said.

Moonlight touched Darla's blond hair and ignited in golden fire. She spoke without turning around, keeping her voice low. "With reason, dear Angelus. This stream is harder to ford than we expected, more treacherous and much longer. There is no place to run, no place to hide. Not even a good place to make a stand. And make no mistake; those men are going to catch Darius and his pirates before they get clear of these mountains."

Ahead of them, one of Darius's men slipped on the bank as loose earth twisted out from underfoot. The pirate landed in the stream, immediately caught in the rush of water and washed downstream before he could get his feet under him. Another of the pirates farther back waded in a short distance and grabbed the man by the shirt, hauling him safely to shore.

"But they won't catch us," Darla promised. "I have a plan."

Long, anxious minutes later Angelus glanced back at the valley mouth they'd entered. The mounted warriors had reached the passage, bunching up to confer over the crash of the racing stream. They talked only a short time, then one of them took the lead and the others followed.

Peering ahead, Angelus saw the fear-filled faces of the vampire pirates looking back to see the mounted warriors.

Even when the horses slipped from the narrow, treacherous banks, the warrior band managed to gain ground. A man, even a vampire, couldn't have stood easily against the current, but the heavier horses with their four legs instead of two, managed.

The animals seemed as driven by the men. Still, one of them did slip and fall, buoyed by the stream and pushed back a dozen yards before it regained its feet. The rider never lost his hold on the horse's mane and quickly pulled himself back into the saddle.

The resilience of their pursuers was eerie. Angelus was beginning to believe for himself they were more than human.

Angelus stared ahead and saw only the continuing wall of rock and scrub brush on either side of the stream. Even climbing with a vampire's strength and agility wouldn't put them out of reach of the warriors in time.

Darla pointed at a short, gnarled tree that had somehow managed to grow on the steep mountainside. "There, Angelus. There is our salvation."

Twisted and warped, the tree still managed to flourish, providing a cluster of branches that made the bank hard to pass at that point. The pirates hacked at branches with their swords but still had to crawl under the main trunk to keep going forward.

"The tree?" Angelus asked.

"Yes." When she reached the tree, Darla took Angelus by the hand and pulled him down to pass under the tree. Only she didn't continue onto the bank. She stepped into the stream, up to her waist in the rushing water within the space of two quick strides. She picked up a stone twice as large as her head and held it within her arms. "Grab a stone. Quickly." She looked back at the approaching warriors.

Still puzzled over what Darla planned, Angelus picked up a rock. When he turned, he found she'd waded even farther out into the stream, up to her chin now.

"Come on," she told him. "The shadow cast by the tree hides us from them for now. That won't last long."

Angelus waded into the water after her. The weight of the massive stone took away the buoyancy that normally would have betrayed him. He didn't stand easily in the current, but he stood. The ice-cold water chilled even him, making his jaws ache.

"Hold on to the rock and go under," Darla suggested. "See if you can walk to the other side of the stream. The water in the deepest part of the channel may be too fast, but get out there as far as you can. If we're lucky, the river will hide us."

Angelus wasn't happy with her plan at all. The water was too cold and too fast, and it was no place to be in a fight. "And if we're not lucky?"

"Drop the rock and leap into the current. It will carry us downstream too fast for them to follow."

"We could get broken and battered on those rocks," Angelus protested.

"Better than getting staked." Following her own advice, Darla walked into the stream and disappeared underwater.

Cursing, Angelus glanced back at the line of advancing warriors. Some of them had lit lanterns and the bull's-eyes glowed like baby moons. Taking a tighter grip on the stone, he waded into the current and let it close over his head. As a vampire, he no longer needed to breathe.

Underwater, he saw Darla before him. The night and the loss of moonlight reflected back on the water reduced her to a silhouette. The current raced across him, tugging at him like a spoiled child in a tantrum. The stream wrapped him in its cold embrace, driving sand and other flotsam into him with stinging force.

The warriors remained vague shapes as they

closed on the tree. The horses hesitated about stepping into the deeper water, but finally did.

Darla continued across the stream and made it to the other side. Still, she remained underwater. Her eyes held green-blue luminosity as she watched him.

In the deepest part of the channel Angelus momentarily lost traction. The stream swept him from his feet with hurried abandon, flinging him around effortlessly for a moment.

Instinctively he curled around the stone he held and sank to the bottom. Once he had his feet under him, he steadied himself and looked for Darla. She was almost twenty feet farther upstream. Resolutely Angelus moved more slowly and gradually gained the shallows. He remained underwater, making his way back to Darla's side.

On the other side of the stream, the warriors continued to negotiate the tree-infested bank with relative ease. The lanterns marked their passage plainly, throwing their immense shadows against the high mountain wall behind them.

Darius and his pirates won't be getting away tonight, Angelus thought. The demon that dwelt inside him now laughed at the misfortune of the other vampires. It didn't matter to him that if it hadn't been for Darla's quick thinking he'd have been in as much trouble as they were.

The shadows of the mounted riders flickered and warred across the lamplit mountainside as the conflicting lantern lights shifted and changed. Silver light gleamed from the bands around their fingers, doubtless the rings that Darius had seen earlier.

Then lantern light spilled across one of the riders, flashing on the red-gold hair pulled back over a shoulder. The rider was on the other side of the tree now, and his vision remained blocked. But the red-gold hair shone through for a moment more.

Hatred and anger filled Angelus as he quietly surfaced. It took all of his strength not to go after the woman after everything she had done to him. But a tingle of fear ran through him, letting him know he wasn't sure he could kill her.

Darla surfaced beside him. "I put a ball into her chest," she whispered insistently. "Anything human would have died."

Angelus watched the last pale yellow light of the warriors' lanterns fade from sight. Once it was gone, he led Darla away, feeling the weight of his sodden clothes. Her words kept playing over again and again in his mind.

Anything human would have died.

But she wasn't human anymore. Even from the distance he'd been able to see that in her.

CHAPTER THIRTEEN

The tall man in black casually strolled across the parking area. His shoes clicked lightly against the pavement. He kept the pistol in his hand but crossed his wrists before him, shielding it with his coat. He appeared totally relaxed. His cold gray eyes never wavered from Angel.

Angel glanced around the parking area.

"No," the gray-haired man said. "I didn't come alone."

"Maybe not," Angel said, "but I bet I can get to you before your friends can stop me."

A small smile twisted the man's lips. "Is it Angelus? Or should I call you Angel now?"

Angel didn't answer.

"However the case may be," the man said in a harsher voice, "I give you the benefit of the doubt. I only today learned that you'd been given your soul back. Congratulations. I suggest that you hold on to it a little more carefully this time."

"Who are you?" Angel demanded.

"You may call me Father Gannon."

"I don't see any vestments, Father," Angel said.

"Nor do I see any evidence of this soul you're reported to have." Gannon shifted the pistol in his hands. "I suppose we'll have to trust each other."

"You're trying to kill Whitney Tyler."

"No," Gannon said softly. "We strive to lay to rest the thing that masquerades itself as Whitney Tyler. She is not human."

Angel gave no indication that he already knew that. "Then what is she?"

"None of your concern," Gannon said. "That's what I came here to tell you. That, and to meet with our brother who has been incarcerated in this dismal establishment."

"Perhaps he's doing penance," Angel suggested.

The glacial gray eyes bored in on his like twin drills. "We know who you are, Angelus. We knew it shortly after Gunnar Schend contacted you. Over the centuries of your life, we've tried to find you."

Angel guessed that it was true. While he'd still been gripped by the vampire's hunger, he'd been on several hunting lists, including the Council of Watchers.

When he'd first gotten his soul back from the

gypsy curse, he'd almost died. It was harder to live while trying not to kill those who attacked him. Whistler had taught him how to hide.

"You're still a vampire," Gannon said. "Several members of my team would like nothing more than to see you staked."

Angel remained silent. He couldn't blame them based on the things he'd done in his past.

"But, at present, we choose to give you the benefit of the doubt."

"Why are you after Whitney?" Angel asked.

"We are responsible for her," Gannon stated simply. "We want what is best."

"And the best thing for her is being dead?"

"Yes."

Angel thought furiously, trying to find a weakness in the man's confidence. "What makes you so sure she's the monster you're after?"

"My . . . organization . . . has been after her for hundreds of years," Gannon said. "That is very privileged information, by the way, and I give it to you now only because your actions since you've been involved in this thing have seemed honorable. We believe strongly in salvation and redemption ourselves. But if you step out of line, we know where you are."

"If your organization has been after her that long," Angel challenged, "why have they only found her now?"

"Because she is very good at hiding." Gannon eyed him levelly. "We've found her a few times in the past, as well as the trail of bodies she left behind. Part of her is a cold-blooded killer, and that part thrives on the savagery that comes so naturally to her. She has succeeded in eluding most of those who followed her, and killing others. Her crimes against the higher power have continued to mount, as has the guilt my organization has assumed over those years."

"What if you have the wrong woman?" Angel asked.

Gannon shook his head. "We don't." He turned to go, then hesitated. "Angelus. *Angel.* I see more compassion in your eyes than I have in any of your kind—and trust me when I say I've staked my share of fiends over the years—but don't let this newfound humanity of yours cloud your judgment. Right and wrong exist in this world. Don't cover those things with moral ambiguity because your own history is cluttered and confusing."

"I've talked to Whitney," Angel said in a more forceful voice. "She's scared and she's an innocent."

"An innocent?" Gannon seemed genuinely amused. "And how would you know innocence? As an appetizer or a main course?"

"Whitney isn't whatever it is you're looking for," Angel said.

"Personal involvement isn't professional," Gannon said. "You've barely met her and already you believe in her."

"No," Angel argued. "I believe in me, and right now everything in me is screaming out that woman's innocence."

Gannon's gray eyes glittered coldly. "Fascinating. A soul and conscience dialed directly in to guilt. At some later point, should you survive the resolution of your obvious course of action in this matter, I would like to talk to you."

"I'll stop you," Angel promised. "No matter what it takes, no matter what I have to do, I'll stop you."

"Is it that easy to slip back into taking human life?"

"In all species," Angel said, "there are some that are easier to destroy because they act out of evil."

"Am I evil, then?"

"Anyone who destroys innocence," Angel said, "is evil by definition and design. It doesn't matter if that person serves a devil or a god. Step up against Whitney Tyler and in my book you're evil."

"I'm not," Gannon said, "in mine." He walked away without another word, moving unhurriedly to the elevator doors and stepping inside. The doors closed before he turned around.

❖   ❖   ❖

"You know what I think she needs?" Cordelia stood in Whitney Tyler's portable makeup trailer.

Whitney and the makeup specialist, a guy named Pete who had so many piercings in his face—*and probably other parts of his anatomy,* Cordelia thought—that an industrial magnet would have ripped him from his feet.

Pete shook his peroxide locks, light glinting from all the metal in his face. He held a makeup brush in one hand and a palette in the other. "She doesn't need anything. She's perfect." He pointed with the brush. "That's gotta be one of the easiest faces to work with I've ever seen in this business."

Whitney looked at her. Once it had gotten dark, and she'd noticed that Angel wasn't around, Whitney had gotten clingy, which was grating on Cordelia's nerves.

Cordelia really didn't blame the woman—much. The kind of nervousness Whitney was exhibiting was probably normal except for firefighters, daredevils, policemen, air-traffic controllers, and graduates of Sunnydale High. School at Sunnydale hadn't been an adventure; it had been a survival course.

"What do you think?" Whitney asked.

"I think you need a *grr* face," Cordelia said honestly.

Pete glanced at her in disbelief. "What are you talking about?"

"She's a vampire, right?" Cordelia asked. "In her show she doesn't have a *grr* face."

"And what exactly is a *grr* face?"

"It's how vampires look when they get all worked up," Cordelia replied. "They get this blend of really ugly creepiness with a lot of stomach churn thrown in." She raised her eyebrows expectantly.

Pete just stared at her.

Someone knocked on the open door of the portable trailer and a young woman stuck her head in. "We need you to be ready on the set in five minutes, Whitney."

Seven minutes later Pete deemed Whitney worthy of returning to the set.

Cordelia walked with the woman. She stared out at the cleared section of the street. The director and his crew had strung the street with cameras that provided a variety of shots and angles where the action would take place. They'd shut down a two-block stretch in front of Hannigan's. Police officers cordoned off the area at all four intersections. A large crowd had formed on the other side of the police cars and sawhorses; people were still excited about the magic of television and movies.

"Where's Angel?" Whitney asked. "I thought he'd be here by now."

"Angel's working for you wherever he is," Cordelia assured her.

"Do you think something happened to Angel?" Whitney asked.

Cordelia frowned. "Well, there is that whole thing about someone trying to kill you, remember? Does 'dead security guard piñata' strike a chord somewhere?"

"That sounds coldhearted."

"Which part?" Cordelia responded. "You asking, or me refusing to tell you what you want to hear, that everything is just hunky-dory? I'm supposed to just deal with the possibility of something happening to Angel all on my own without you claiming any share of it?" She shook her head. "Nope. Not interested."

"You're right," Whitney said. "I'm sorry."

"And if you think copping that poor-me pose and—" Cordelia stopped, open-mouthed. "Did you just apologize?"

"Yes."

"Oh." Cordelia closed her mouth.

Despite her tension, Whitney laughed. "I don't think I've ever met anyone like you."

"Don't feel badly," Cordelia said. "No one else has, either."

"I just wish he was here," Whitney said. "I feel safe around him."

Cordelia nodded in agreement as they walked toward the middle intersection in the two blocks. Two cars were parked in the center of the intersection.

"I feel safer, too," Cordelia admitted. "I'm used to taking care of myself, but sometimes—when things have been a little bit more than I can handle, which by the way, is almost never—it makes me feel good to know he's there. Granted, most days with too much time spent around him while he's off on a major brood is no picnic. There are days when he makes Eeyore look like Pollyanna."

"Who's Eeyore?" Whitney asked.

"Uh-oh," Cordelia said, "somebody didn't have a Disney childhood."

"I've seen Disney," Whitney said. "I just can't place Eeyore."

"He was a stuffed donkey, kind of like Grumpy in *Snow White*. Eeyore was one of Winnie the Pooh's friends in the Big Woods." Cordelia paused. "Or maybe Laura Ingalls lived there. I get them confused."

"Laura Ingalls is the name of a donkey too?"

"No. Laura Ingalls of *Little House on the Prairie*."

"Sorry. Don't know that one, either."

"How did you ever make it into television if you don't know these things?"

Whitney laughed. "I never planned on starring in television when I grew up."

A well-built guy in a blue fire-retardant jumpsuit turned toward Whitney with a clipboard in his hands. He kept his head shaved and wore a short beard. "Hey, Whitney, how are you doing?"

"I'm fine, Mike." Whitney made introductions quickly. "Mike Zohn, meet Cordelia Chase. Cordelia, this is Mike, our stunt coordinator for the series."

They shook hands and Zohn turned toward Whitney, his face somber. "What happened last night, kid, it's all over the news. I'm sorry."

Whitney nodded. "Thanks."

Zohn gave Whitney all his attention. "I don't know why Schend wants you here for this shoot, kid. We could have ran this with a stand-in in a wig."

Whitney pointed at a sign over a nearby building. In the afternoon it had been a shoe store. Now, with the false front bolted into place, it passed as a Hollings Computer Solutions business office.

"Because Hollings was promised my face in front of that," Whitney said.

Zohn shrugged. "Could have blue screened it in. Nobody would have known."

"Hollings would have known."

"He's got those deep pockets."

"I know, and Gunnar's trying to get his arm in them up to the elbow."

Zohn nodded. "It's just the biz, kid. We'll go over your marks, get you through this gag and out safely."

"Okay."

Cordelia watched as Zohn led Whitney down the street. As she watched the actress, Cordelia was surprised to find that she felt a little sorry for her. Until Whitney had mentioned never knowing Winnie the Pooh and Eeyore—never big stars in Cordelia's life, although she could remember an extravagance of attention from her parents during that time—Cordelia hadn't really thought about all the things the woman had missed out on.

So where had Whitney Tyler's childhood gone?

CHAPTER FOURTEEN

"I need a favor," Angel said. They sat in Kate Lockley's car at the side of the street in front of Angel's offices. He felt bad about asking. Bad twice, actually, because what Kate was going to do could potentially hurt someone he was trying to protect.

"What's the favor?" she asked

"I need to know what the background check on Whitney turns up."

"You don't do that?" Kate flashed him a surprised look.

"I've got a computer and access to the archived news services, but I don't have resources into the government databases that you do," Angel admitted. "Usually I can make do with that. And if I felt I had more time, I wouldn't ask because I can get what I need eventually. But I want this done in-depth and quickly. And without a lot of other people knowing. I trust you."

Kate flipped up the sun visor with the mirror and turned to look at him. "Okay. You've got my attention, but someday we're going to have to talk about what it is you do and who it is you help."

"The people I help," Angel replied, "generally don't have problems coming out of the past. They're just trying to live through today to get to tomorrow."

Kate studied him with her gaze. "You're hooked, aren't you?" she asked softly. "On Whitney Tyler?"

"I like her," Angel answered simply. "She doesn't deserve to be treated the way she is. There's something vulnerable about her."

"You wouldn't know it the way she kicks the major bad guy's butt every week on the show."

Angel smiled. "Probably not."

"What do you need me to dig into exactly?" Kate asked.

Angel hesitated for a moment. "I don't know."

Surprise lifted Kate's eyebrows. "Maybe you're not as hooked on her as I thought."

Angel made no reply.

"Are you sure you want to do that?" Kate asked.

"I'm sure I don't want to do that," Angel told her honestly. "But I'm also sure it's what I have to do."

Doyle sat in the little antechamber in the back of the Chinese laundry and tried not to move too much. Moving meant calling attention from the huge Mongol warrior that guarded the door to Yuan's private chambers. And it looked like Mama Ntombi's suggestion that he set up the meeting so he could find out more information was a total bust. There were no big arrows, no big signs. No clues.

The Mongol yawned but didn't look tired. It was boredom setting in.

Comes from not lopping off toes today, right? Doyle hoped that was true. He kept checking the painted cement floor for bloodstains. Shoes weren't exactly designed to hold in body fluids, and blood had a tendency to run everywhere.

He'd been sitting there for more than an hour, his mind inanely and incessantly chanting lines from the original *Snow White*. In that version the evil stepsisters had chopped up their feet to fit into the glass slipper the Prince's men brought around.

One of them had cut off her big toe, hoping for a shot at being princess. Only the sparrows had warned the Prince as he'd ridden off with his bride-to-be. *Prithee, prithee, look back, look back! There's blood on the track!* And sure enough, there had been. The two stepsisters had been delivered back to their mom, a couple shoe sizes smaller and no crown in sight.

Doyle looked at the Mongol. The man looked

almost six and a half feet tall and nearly half as wide. He wore his hair long, his chin decorated with a Fu Manchu mustache and little sprig of a beard. The Sheryl Crow concert T-shirt looked stretched to the ripping point. Black, gathered ankle commando pants and Doc Martens completed his wardrobe. The massive hand cannon parked under his left arm was obviously more than an accessory.

Three people had come out of the room since Doyle had been waiting. Only one of them had been limping, but Doyle couldn't rightly remember if the man had been limping when he arrived, so he still didn't know how things were going.

Yuan called out on the other side of the door, speaking Cantonese.

The Mongol curled a finger at Doyle. "Let's go."

Doyle stood and submitted to the frisk the big warrior put him through, then followed the door into Yuan's private office. The smell of cherry-blend incense immediately cloyed his nose and reminded him of the grocery store.

The small desk, executive chair, and straight-backed chair in front of it nearly filled the tiny room. Yuan sat behind the desk, a gray-haired man with stylish glasses dressed in a neatly pressed white shirt and black tie. The beads on the abacus he used for calculations clacked rapidly as he moved them. Besides the clack of the abacus beads, only the laundry's day-to-day clank and grind sounded in the room, muted by the concrete block walls.

Yuan glanced up unexpectedly. Surprisingly, the old man smiled. "Mr. Doyle."

"Yeah," Doyle said, wishing afterward he could have just kept his big mouth closed. "That's me."

Yuan consulted a small leather-bound notebook in front of him. "It appears you owe me money."

Always owing somebody, Doyle thought with self-disgust. *And we all know the chorus on that one.* "Yeah, guess I do."

"And quite a tidy sum, it appears." Yuan glanced up. "Do you have the money?"

"Not all of it," Doyle replied. There'd been Madame Ntombi's fee, plus the couple stiff drinks he'd had next door to get the courage to come here. Plus, he hadn't had all that much to begin with. "You will get your money. I guarantee that. I've never welched on a bet in my life."

Yuan consulted his small book again. "Actually, Mr. Doyle, it appears that you've neglected to pay a few of your gambling debts. I could make most of the money back that I cannot get from you by simply holding you here for other entrepreneurs such as myself. There are several that appear simply willing to make an example of you at this juncture."

Cold fear closed in on Doyle, but it came with a taste of anger. "You just found all that out?"

"On the contrary," Yuan replied, "I've known for weeks. I also know that you occasionally frequented the tavern next door." The bookie steepled his hands. "I have been waiting for you."

"Man, now that sounds completely foolhardy on your part." Doyle grinned, then noticed that Yuan wasn't smiling and dropped the humor. "I mean, if you don't mind my saying so."

"It was a plan," Yuan replied, "and a hope that the gods of chance would favor me."

"To place a bet with me?" Doyle couldn't believe it.

"To place a bet with you that you would lose," Yuan replied. "And hope that you were not able to pay it off."

"I'm telling you, that's just not good business." Doyle figured things were so weird that he might as well say what he wanted to say.

"But your needs are not mine." Yuan pushed the pile of crumpled bills Doyle had placed on the desk at the end of his story toward the half-demon. "In fact, I would prefer if you kept the whole amount."

Stunned, Doyle dropped into the chair in front of the desk. "If you don't mind me asking, what do you get out of this deal?"

Yuan reached into the desk drawer and brought out one of the Angel Investigations cards. He flipped it in his manicured fingers. "You are with the detective, yes? The one who stalks the shadows of this city?"

Doyle thought the description sounded moxie. "Angel? Yeah, I'm kind of partnered up with him."

"So I've been told." Yuan took out a pen and quickly wrote on the back. "This is my personal phone number. I can be reached here at any time. I would like your partner to call me at his earliest convenience on a matter of some urgency."

"You want Angel to do a job for you?" Doyle asked.

"Yes."

"Angel isn't the one who owes you money," Doyle said. "And if you read the card closely, you'll see that we help the helpless. Says so down at the bottom. Angel's not really going to like the idea of toe collecting from some poor guy who doesn't have the money to pay you."

"It's not like that."

"You mean you really do collect toes?" Even though he'd been told that and after all the other weirdness he'd seen—and lived through—Doyle still struggled to believe that.

Yuan reached beneath the desk and brought out a gallon jar.

Doyle tried hard not to look too closely at the spherical shapes that bobbed in the heavy liquid. "I can't believe you do that."

Yuan shrugged. "They are only toes. Not much use except as reminders that promises made are promises that should be kept." He put the gallon jar back out of sight. "And in this matter where I need Angel's services, I am helpless."

"Maybe I can try to help you," Doyle suggested. "After all, the debt is mine."

"If I had to rely only on your help," Yuan stated, "I'd rather have my money. Perhaps a toe."

"Okay." Doyle nodded agreeably. "Angel usually sees things my way. With a little help. Tell me what you need, and I'll see if I can convince him."

"I will talk to Angel when I see him."

Doyle saw from the bookie's steely gaze that the only deal he was going to get was on the table. "All right, I'm good with that. You need me to run messages, I'm a hell of a message runner."

"When can I see Angel?" Yuan pressed.

"I'll have to get with him," Doyle said. "Find out what his schedule is. That sort of thing."

Yuan was silent for a moment. "I'll see him tomorrow. In the evening. I understand he doesn't much care for business during the day."

"Not much," Doyle agreed.

Yuan stood behind the desk and bowed. "Then

our business this night has been concluded satis-
factorily by both of us."

Doyle stood as well, then turned to the door and
knocked. The Mongol warrior opened the door to
let him out. He glanced at the other man sitting in
the chair he'd left only minutes ago, feeling sorry
for the poor slob.

Then he realized the poor slob was Gunnar
Schend.

Schend looked totally blown away. "Hey," he
croaked. "Fancy meeting you here." His unctuous
smile didn't quite come off and looked like it
would be more at home on someone having terrible gas pains.

"Aren't you supposed to be at the evening
shoot?" Doyle asked.

Schend hooked a thumb at Yuan's door. "I've got
to see Mr. Yuan about . . . an on-site location he
owns." The television producer got up from the
chair and walked to the door when the Mongol
warrior motioned him inside.

"Yeah," Doyle said. "I had to talk to him myself.
They're putting too much starch in the collars
again."

Schend waved and disappeared inside the room.

Doyle looked at the bodyguard. "He's not here
about an on-site location, is he?"

The big man shook his head.

"I didn't think so."

"Mr. Yuan wanted you to know," the Mongol warrior stated. "He scheduled the man here so you would see him because he knew your friend was working on the case with the actress."

"How did Yuan know?" Doyle asked.

"Mr. Yuan makes it his business to know things. For this thing, Mr. Yuan needed to know about your friend. So he learned. And in doing so, he learned about you. Letting you know about this man's gambling habits is a favor in advance for the favor you are going to do him."

Doyle ran his hand through his hair, thinking, putting the pieces together. Maybe he wasn't a real detective, but a guy didn't exactly have to be Sherlock Holmes to smell a rat here.

"Tell Mr. Yuan thanks," Doyle said.

"All right, people, let's get this in one. Action."

Cordelia stood behind the barricade the stunt-man rescue squad had set up to run the gag. The stuntmen and women around her laughed and joked, sipping coffee or fruit drinks. It was another day of work for them. Cordelia felt as if she had a snake crawling through her stomach.

Whitney had no place on the set with everything that was going on. But Schend had insisted, partly because of Hollings's interest and partly because in light of the murder, most of the entertainment news networks were out in full force. Sending in a double was out of the question.

At the north end of the two-block stretch of street, a stuntman splashed a chemical concoction across the front of a Trans Am that was supposed to try to run Honor Blaze down in the street. Whitney Tyler stood on the other end of the second block, on the side of the street across from the stunt barricade. She didn't look nervous at all.

"Why are they going to set the car on fire?" Cordelia asked the rawboned stuntwoman standing next to her.

The woman shrugged. "The director or the writer. One of them decided it would look cool, a flaming car hurtling down on Whitney. So we burn it. Makes doing the gag easier because we don't have to worry about doing cuts for the close-ups. With the flames blazing, no one will be able to see into the car. Mike can wear more protective gear."

When the stuntman finished sloshing the liquid across the front of the Trans Am, he stepped back. "All ready."

"Okay!" the director shouted back over the PA system that rolled thunder along the street. "We do it in one, people. Hit your marks. And . . . action!"

Whitney Tyler stepped out onto the street when the rigged lights turned green. At the same time a voice behind her demanded, "Bud, what the hell's going on?"

Drawn by Mike Zohn's voice, Cordelia turned.

The stuntman leader stood in front of the portable dressing trailer dressed only in a pair of boxers. A lump on the side of his left temple looked as big as a kiwi fruit.

"Hey," Cordelia said, "you're supposed to be driving that car out there."

"I got news for you, sister," Zohn growled. "I'm not driving that car."

"Well, someone is," a stuntwoman said. "And whoever it is has got your outfit on."

"Somebody knocked me out in the dressing room," Zohn complained. "Big guy."

Cordelia turned and glanced out at the street. Whitney Tyler was halfway across. "Whitney!" she shouted. "It's one of those fruitcakes after Whitney!" She dashed from behind the barricade.

At the end of the block the gaffer lit the liquid. The clinging, incendiary film caught in a rush of blue and yellow flames that quickly shifted more toward violent red. Rubber shrilled when the car shot forward, snarling like some homicidal beast.

Cordelia saw instantly that neither she nor the stunt crew was going to reach Whitney before the car roared over her. She shouted at the actress, waving her back.

Then Whitney saw them. She stood frozen for a moment, her gaze torn between the stunt crew and the Trans Am hurtling at her while wreathed in flames. At the last moment, she leaped aside. Cordelia would have sworn the wind-spun flames must have licked across her body.

Just as Cordelia was starting to relax, thinking the driver would attempt to escape, the car brakes shrilled. Incredibly, the Trans Am slewed around in a tight one-eighty, losing ground for a moment like a cat on ice. Then the tires found traction, and the car shot forward.

Cordelia watched as the vehicle closed on Whitney. The actress was only now getting to her feet. There was no way she could avoid being run down. The car raced at her, the fire clinging to the front of it and looking like a gaping mouth below the wide-lensed eye of the windshield.

CHAPTER FIFTEEN

The flaming car roared at Whitney Tyler. The actress stood frozen, like a deer caught in the sudden glare of headlights.

Just before she turned away so she wouldn't have to see the impact, Cordelia spotted a figure dressed in black in her peripheral vision. "Angel," she whispered, feeling more hopeful. Then she remembered the flames wrapped around the Trans Am could kill him, too.

Angel ran faster than anything human, his arms swinging at his sides as he drove his feet against the ground. His long duster trailed out behind him. Without breaking stride, he slowed only enough to shove Whitney out of the way of the speeding car, but he didn't have time to get clear himself.

Cordelia watched, certain she was about to witness Angel's death. Only this time there wouldn't be any coming back.

Incredibly, Angel didn't try to turn away from the approaching car. Still in motion, he leaped onto the flaming car hood. As soon as his feet touched down, they were yanked out from under him by the speeding car.

Even though she'd seen Angel and Buffy pull off incredible moves before, Cordelia still watched in awe as Angel spun over the speeding car. He landed on his feet on the street and almost kept his balance, but gravity won out over vampiric strength, speed, and skill. He fell to one side, sprawling ungracefully across the street.

The man driving the Trans Am tried to pull the vehicle around again, but the fire had spread to the tires. They exploded only a heartbeat apart in sudden rushes. Black smoke roiled from the charring rubber. Sparks shot out from the pavement as the rims ate through the weakened treads and scraped.

Out of control, the car slammed into the front of Hannigan's. Glass emptied from the bar's windows, showering down on the vehicle. The flames leaped up from the car to sink hungry fangs into the awning above.

"Go!" Zohn ordered.

The stunt team raced forward with fire extinguishers.

"Cordelia!"

Turning, Cordelia spotted Angel helping Whitney to her feet. Cordelia ran across the street and took the actress's other hand, draping her arm across her shoulders.

"Can you handle her?" Angel asked.

"Yeah."

"Don't let her out of your sight," Angel said.

"I won't," Cordelia replied. "I was trained for this. Sort of. And how hard is it to lose a person?"

Angel's face showed a momentary flicker of past pain. "Too easy." In the next instant he was gone, sprinting toward the wrecked car where the driver was trying to start the engine.

Cordelia looked at Whitney, noting the dazed look in her eyes. *Maybe it's a concussion.* At Sunnydale High everyone had gotten a crash course in becoming a triage. Dead or alive? Gonna live or gonna die? Regular blood flow or arterial?

Scanning her quickly, Cordelia didn't find any wounds that immediately needed attention. Twin holes in the neck were always the first on the list. Sucking chest wounds a close second. But Whitney did have scratches on the side of her neck and one of her arms. None of the scratches was very deep.

Taking the woman's waist, Cordelia helped her

limp toward the sidewalk. "You're going to be okay," she said. "Everything's going to be okay."

"Angel Investigations. We help the helpless. If that's you, leave a message at the beep." The answering machine in the office beeped. Doyle liked listening to Cordelia's voice. Sometimes in the middle of the night when he was in his apartment, he'd call just to listen to her. He told himself that wasn't pathetic or abnormal.

He stood at the pay phone just inside Winkle's, his head stuck out the door so he could watch Gunnar Schend's Hummer parked in front of the Chinese laundry. "Look, it's me," he told the answering machine. "I think I'm on to something here. I'm at Winkle's, the bar next to the Chinese laundry. While I was there paying my respects— and other stuff—to Yuan, guess who I happened to run into?"

The answering machine hissed sedately in his ear for a moment, not guessing at all.

"Well, okay, don't guess," Doyle went on. "If Gunnar Schend happens to cross your mind while you're listening to this, you win. I'm going to tag along behind him. You see, it occurs to me that only Whitney and Gunnar knew where she was last night. And the security guards. But I don't think the one would have chosen to get himself killed.

Of course, that's me just thinking out loud here. And the other guard looked scared spitless."

The cab Doyle had put on standby idled at the curb.

"It stands to reason that if these guys didn't just get lucky and find her, someone had to tell them where she was. And if they're that lucky, I'm grabbing one of them and taking them Off Track Betting before the police lock them up and throw away the key. By the way, the group that we're after—the ones who belong to the symbol—are called the Blood Cadre. They're a band of demon hunters who've been around for about the last five hundred years. The way I hear it, they're not a bunch you want mad at you."

Gunner Schend emerged from the laundry and walked quickly to his Hummer. *Must have gone well,* Doyle thought. *He's not limping.* The locking mechanism warbled and the interior lights flashed on.

"Well, we're on the move," Doyle said. "I'll try to call you from wherever it is we land. But I'm betting after this meeting with Yuan, Schend may need a cash fix." He cradled the phone and walked out to the cab.

"That the guy?" the driver asked as Doyle slid into the cab's rear seat.

"Yeah," Doyle replied. *Like there were a dozen*

*other Hummers parked in front of the Chinese
laundry.* "Don't lose him."

The heat of the burning car washed over Angel.
Men and women carrying fire extinguishers were
on his heels. White foam fire retardant sprayed
from the funnel mouths, hosing the car.

Clad in a Nomex fireproof mask with goggle
lenses and a black Nomex bodysuit, the driver
looked alien. The goggles focused on Angel, but he
didn't stop trying to start the car. The starter
ground like claws scraping concrete. The flames
spreading across the car stood up against the fire
extinguisher assault.

"Get back!" one of the men commanded. "We're
losing the car! When those flames hit the gas tank,
it's going to blow!"

The firefighters dodged back.

"Mickey, Bob! Get the people in the bar away
from the front of the building!"

Angel grabbed the car door handle. Heat seared
his palm, but he kept his grip. He put a foot against
the car body and ripped the door out of the frame.
Then he reached in and hauled the driver out.

The man tried to fight, but Angel gave him no
chance at all. He backhanded the man, sending
him stumbling a couple steps backward till he
tripped.

Angel was on the man before he could get up. The Nomex suit smoked and felt almost hot enough to burn when Angel gripped the chest in one fist. He ripped the goggle-eyed mask off with his other hand.

The man was in his early twenties, sporting cold eyes and a hard, brittle mouth. His hair was as red as blood in the firelight. He hacked and coughed from the smoke in his lungs.

"Give Gannon a message for me," Angel said.

Unable to speak, the man shook his head violently. Red and blue lights added to the mix, whirling over the crowd of television people.

"Tell Gannon to stay away from the woman," Angel ordered. "Tell him to keep all of you people back."

"We can't," the man replied. "She's our responsibility."

"No," Angel stated coldly. "She's *my* responsibility. You tell that to Gannon. And you tell him I said I know that."

Two uniformed police officers approached Angel with drawn weapons. "Back off, pal," one of them said. "We've got him now."

Reluctantly, feeling powerless to stop what he felt certain was coming, Angel released the man and stepped back. He turned away as the police officers rolled the man over and handcuffed him.

Angel peered down the street, spotting Cordelia standing next to Whitney.

"You don't know what she is!" the man shouted after him. "You don't know what she's capable of!"

Angel ignored the man and joined Cordelia and Whitney, who were surrounded by television crew members. Politely but firmly, Angel forced his way through the crowd to Whitney's side.

"We need to get out of here," he told her.

Whitney had her arms wrapped around herself. Her face was ashen gray. "But you caught him."

"There are more," Angel said, taking her by the arm.

The television crew pressed in around them, asking question after question.

"We're leaving," Angel said. "We're taking Whitney somewhere safe. If she needs any of you, she'll be in touch."

"That's right," Cordelia added. "Angel Investigations is on the case. We help the helpless. If that's you, give us a call."

Angel took the lead again, walking over to the private parking lot that had been rented by the studio for the day. He guided Whitney to his car parked at the curb.

"Wait," Whitney said in a dulled voice. "My car's over there. I need some things out of it. Sleeping in one of your shirts the last time might have been okay, but I want some of my things this time." She looked at Angel, noticing the hesitation in him.

More than anything, Angel wanted to go. There was too much attention, too many people, and more things that could go wrong than he could handle.

"Please," Whitney said. "These people have taken my life away. Don't let them take everything."

Angel nodded, knowing he didn't want either Cordelia or Whitney out of his sight. Gannon's people were finding Whitney Tyler way too easily. "Okay. But we're going together. Where's your car?"

Whitney pointed. "Gunnar got a driver for me who was supposed to stay with it."

Two security guards stood at the checkpoint onto the lot. "What's going on over there?" one of the men asked.

The fire from the burning car had lit up the streets, throwing smoke high into the sky. Red and blue flashing slights strobed without pause from the police cruisers.

"They're shooting a television show," Cordelia answered.

The older man shook his head. "They didn't say anything about a fire that big."

"Supposed to be a surprise," Cordelia said. "Are you surprised?"

"Yeah." Neither of the security guards appeared happy about it.

Whitney took a key from her pocket as they neared the Mercedes sedan. She pressed the clicker, and the horn bleated as the interior light came on, revealing the man slumped in the driver's seat.

Whitney had her hand on the rear door handle when Angel saw the blood covering the driver's chest. He bent low and peered inside.

"Wait," he whispered, taking her hand in his.

The driver's head lay to the side, the angle suggesting that the skull had been separated from the spine. One of his eyes stared sightlessly through the windshield; the other lay on his cheek, gouged from the socket. His throat had been ripped out deep enough to expose the spine at the back. A card with the strange symbol and the word *atonement* written on it was stuck to the corpse's bloody chest.

"What is it?" Whitney asked. Then she looked at the driver. Her hand formed a fist inside Angel's.

"Is he passed out drunk or something?" Cordelia asked from behind them.

Angel turned to her. "He's dead." He took the keys from Whitney's hand and locked the car again. The interior light followed them for a moment as they retreated to his car. He watched the shadows in the parking lot, wondering if whatever had killed the driver was still there. Then the car's interior light winked out.

"You folks find everything okay?" one of the guards asked.

"Yeah, thanks," Angel said. He lowered his voice. "Don't stop moving." He watched as the two guards talked, then one of them walked toward the Mercedes and took out his flashlight.

"Maybe we should walk a little faster," Cordelia suggested.

Angel held the door open for both women. He was rounding the back of his car when the guard checking the car cursed loudly and backed away from the Mercedes. Angel stepped onto the back bumper of his car and leaped into the driver's seat. The last thing he wanted was a chat session with the LAPD.

Putting his foot down hard on the accelerator, Angel shot through the city, trying to figure out what he was going to do next, hoping he was wrong about the dark suspicion that had taken root in his mind.

"This is close enough," Doyle told the cab driver. He peered across the nearly empty motor court of the run-down motel.

The tail lights on Gunnar Schend's Hummer flared briefly, then extinguished as the television producer got out. He hesitated briefly, studying the numbers on the door. Then he knocked.

Doyle didn't recognize the gray-haired man who answered the door, but he could tell from Schend's body language that the television producer wasn't totally relaxed with the encounter.

And if he's not relaxed, this deal probably isn't very kosher. Doyle opened the door and stepped out. "Give me a minute here," he told the driver, handing over a ten. "I want to chat with the manager really quick. If the guy in the Hummer decides to leave, wheel over and pick me up at the office."

The driver took the ten and nodded.

Doyle crossed over to the office set up as the first section of the U-shaped motel court. The wrinkled old guy behind the scarred desk and thick plexiglas was watching Letterman, laughing as Dave went through his opening monologue. He glanced up at Doyle.

Taking a twenty dollar bill from his pocket, Doyle spread the paper across the counter just within reach under the plexiglass slot.

The clerk glanced at the twenty and licked his lips, but he didn't get up from his chair. "Something I can do for you?"

"I'd like to know the name of a guest you've got staying here."

The old man shook his head. "I don't think so."

Doyle added another twenty, glancing out quickly to see that the cab was in the same place. He took it as a sign that Schend hadn't moved yet. "It's kind of important to me."

The old man flicked his eyes over the two bills. "It's not important enough to me."

Doyle added another twenty. "I know the guy out there talking to him."

"Ask him."

Another twenty joined the three others. "I kind of want it to be a surprise."

"You a cop?"

"No."

"Planning on doing anything bad to those people?"

"No."

"Why do you want to know?"

Doyle added another bill. "A hundred dollars says I don't have to answer that question."

The old man got up from his creaky chair, unable to maintain interest in the talk show. He gazed hungrily at the stack of bills.

When Doyle spotted the off-track-betting form under the *TV Guide*, the half-demon knew he had the man. "Got a favorite horse?"

The old man squinted up at him. "Maybe."

Doyle shrugged. "It'd be better if you could put some heavy cash down. If you're really feeling lucky, that is." And he knew there was no other way a seasoned gambler would feel. The job at the motel court didn't look like it covered much in the way of off-track betting.

"His name is Derek Gannon," the old man said, after consulting a grease-stained register. He reached for the cash.

Doyle kept his thumb heavily on the stack of bills. "What can you tell me about him?"

"He's some kind of priest or something," the old man said. "I've seen him with crosses, out in the courtyard praying with his friends."

"What friends?"

The clerk's eyes never left the money and his fingers pressed hard against the edges he could touch. "He's got a lot of guys **work**ing with him. They got other rooms here."

"Know who the guy in the black Hummer is?"

The old man shook his head. "I seen him in here a couple times. Comes and goes. Always acting guilty."

"The father and his friends from around here?"

"No. They got accents. British or something."

"What business do they have?"

The old man shrugged. "You want a lot for a hundred bucks."

Doyle smiled. "Makes us even, don't you think? You want a hundred bucks a lot."

"I don't know what they're doing here. They've been here a week. Pay their bills in cash. Don't bother nobody. They must have somebody in jail, though."

"Why do you say that?"

"Gannon came in today and asked me where the county jail was."

"He could have taken a cab."

"He didn't."

Doyle thought about that, remembering that the man who'd tried to run Whitney Tyler down at the diner two days ago had been taken to the county jail. "Thanks, old-timer." He released the money and the clerk swept it away without looking up. He went back to Letterman for the Top Ten list.

Doyle went back out to the cab, arriving about the same time Schend climbed back into the Hummer.

"Want to keep following him?" the cab driver asked.

Doyle watched Schend pull back out onto the street. "No." He gave the man the address to Angel's office. Before he made another move, the half-demon wanted to talk with Angel. With this many people on board and things starting to add up, like Schend wasn't such a good guy where Whitney Tyler was concerned, he wanted to talk strategy.

Angel pushed up the floor covering from the tunnels that ran beneath his office and home, then climbed into the dark room. He'd come along the hidden way even though it was night to lessen his chances of being spotted. He'd counted at least two men in surveillance positions out on the street. If it hadn't been night they wouldn't have stood out so much. The smell of fresh coffee struck him instantly and put him on guard.

"Relax. It's only me." Doyle sat at the table near a carryout tray that had held four coffees in Styrofoam cups. "I called and left messages on the answering machine."

"Cordelia and I found a safehouse to put Whitney up in." Angel left the trapdoor open as he walked over to the bookshelves. He turned on the light, flooding the room with illumination. Since there were no windows to allow the daylight in, the unbroken walls also served to keep the light inside from being seen outside now. "I figured the police would take her into protective custody at the very least."

"After they found her driver dead in the car."

"How did you know about that?" Angel asked.

"News bulletin." Doyle pointed at the television as Angel moved to the bookcase. "At the very least they would have done that. So what are you doing here? When you first put in an appearance, I thought maybe you were coming for me, but now that I see you going through all those books, I have to wonder."

Angel glanced at Doyle. "I came back for you."

"Okay, but what else?"

"I wanted to look up a few things."

"I could help."

"Did you find out anything about that symbol?" Angel asked. His mind still raced, still determined to pursue the dark twisting path it had already started out on.

"They're part of the Blood Cadre," Doyle said. "Dedicated demon hunters one and all."

"Do they wear the symbol on a silver ring?"

Angel stopped flipping through the book on Irish folklore and myth. It dealt predominantly with the Tuatha Du'Dannan, the mystical race all faeries were thought to be descended from.

Doyle pointed at the carryout tray. "Would you like a coffee?"

Angel nodded but didn't comment.

"Have you ever met Mama Ntombi?" Doyle asked.

"No."

"Interesting woman. You really should make time for it."

"The point, Doyle," Angel growled irritably. Time and everything else was working against them.

"And there is one, I assure you." Doyle brought a coffee over. "Anyway, while I'm there, Mama Ntombi triggers a couple visions she lets me see, allowing me a closer look at things I'm generally only guessing at. I'm thinking maybe I should take lessons."

Angel waited.

"In this vision," Doyle went on, "I saw the woman aboard a sailing ship—"

"It was called *Handsome Jack*," Angel said, smelling the salt in the air. "I was there. She was part of the guard surrounding a group of English nobles and wealthy that were coming to Galway back in 1758. The Scottish Rebellion was going on then, and things were going hard on the Catholics again."

"Never a fun time over there, is it?" Doyle flashed him a rueful smile. "Do you know who this woman was?"

"They called her Moira," Angel said evenly, not showing the raw guilt that twisted within him. "I killed her. At least, I thought I had. When she crossed blades with me aboard *Handsome Jack*, I knew I had to have her. I wanted to break her, taste her blood, and look into her eyes as she gave up." The memory was strong within him, causing a confusion of emotions.

"But you didn't," Doyle said. "In my vision I saw her again at a later time."

"No," Angel said, "I didn't. I even thought Darla killed her once, then I convinced myself that Darla had somehow missed her with the pistol or that a ball hadn't been rammed down the barrel."

"And Darla is?"

"My sire. I staked her when she tried to kill Buffy."

"Bad career move on her part," Doyle stated dryly. "But one thing I did notice in this vision was how much that woman then looked like Whitney Tyler now."

A chill filled Angel. "There are differences."

"Right." Doyle sounded totally unconvinced. "So what are you here researching?"

"Ghosts, goblins, the usual."

"Ah, and you believe Whitney Tyler is one of those creatures?"

"Actually, I'm starting to think she's possessed," Angel said. "Do you have that tape you and Cordelia got from the apartment building?"

Doyle vanished upstairs and came back down a

moment later with the tape in his hand. "I didn't know you'd gotten a chance to look at it."

Angel took the tape and plugged it into the TV VCR in the bookshelves. Television wasn't a hobby of his, but he'd found having the setup around was helpful. "I looked at the notes you and Cordelia made last night and noticed a discrepancy."

"In our notes?" Doyle shook his head. "We took very good notes. An attention to detail is the standard definition of a detective."

"Doyle," Angel said patiently, "we're not exactly private eyes. We're here to save people, not figure out whodunit."

"Good," Doyle said, "because that whodunit stuff can really make my head hurt. I mean, take Clue for instance. You can throw off a whole game by—"

"You took good notes." Angel started the VCR player. "Watch." On the television, Whitney Tyler entered the building. "At one-seventeen A.M. Whitney arrives after the attack went down on the highway."

"Yeah, and she got back from shopping at two fifty-eight," Doyle said.

Angel fast-forwarded to the second entrance. Whitney Tyler walked through the foyer again.

Doyle pointed at the time-date stamp. It was 2:58. "There's your time."

"I know," Angel said, reversing the tape in slow motion and watching the segments again. "I just want to know when she left."

Doyle stared at the screen, understanding dawning in his eyes. "She arrived there twice but never left." He ran his hand through his hair. "Maybe the security guy missed it."

"Maybe." Angel shut the machine off. "Help me with these books." He took an armload from the shelf, picking them by title and subject matter. All of them dealt with Irish legends.

Doyle was staggered under the weight. "We're going to carry all of this through the tunnels?"

"It's only about six blocks," Angel replied. "An easy walk."

"But not a happy one," Doyle promised.

Angel put the stack of books he was carrying on the table and started up the stairs.

"Where are you going?" Doyle asked.

"Check the answering machine. I'm expecting a call."

"From Detective Lockley?"

"Yeah."

"You also need to call Bascomb. I had him research the Blood Cadre. I might have been able to find something in your books, but I knew we were pressed for time."

Bascomb was an authority on legends, myths, and magical things in the L.A. area. Angel had heard of him even before he'd made the move to L.A.

"They called," Doyle said. "Wanted you to call back as soon as you could."

CHAPTER SIXTEEN

The phone rang three times before it was answered. "Bascomb."

Angel listened to the cultured tones of the man. "It's Angel."

"Ah, Angel," Bascomb said unctuously. "Your earlier call—combined with the brief fax—being so cryptic, actually, left me rather intrigued."

Angel held a cell phone as he drove past a twenty-four-hour convenience store a few blocks away from his office. Night filled the streets with shadows. He felt certain either the Blood Cadre or the LAPD—and perhaps both—were still watching his offices.

"I caught the news earlier," Bascomb said, "and noticed that a private investigator with the singular name of Angel was linked with a murder attempt against Whitney Tyler, the television star. I couldn't imagine that there would be more than one."

Angel didn't comment.

"Of course, that's probably your business." Bascomb cleared his throat. "I was able to find some material on the Blood Cadre."

"A band of religious demon hunters and kind of obsessive about it."

"To say the least," Bascomb commented. "They were very dedicated to their chosen vocation, and even the Watchers took note of their successes. Secret organizations tend only to be secret from everyone but each other. In the past, the Watchers and the Slayers have had occasional dealings with the Cadre. But I think I found the anomaly you were looking for."

Angel watched the traffic slide by on the other side of the street. *Anomaly,* he thought. *There's a word.*

"There was a young woman who was a member of the Blood Cadre back in 1758, as you suggested," Bascomb went on. "And she was aboard a ship called *Handsome Jack* that was attacked by particularly vicious vampires."

The man's words brought back all the guilt that was associated with Angelus's actions back then. He saw the swordswoman's face again, so like Whitney Tyler's.

"I'm sorry," Bascomb said. "Perhaps I spoke out of turn. I didn't stop to think that—"

That I might have been one of those vicious vampires? "What about the woman?" Angel asked.

"Reports indicated that the new arrivals under"—papers rustled again for a moment—"a man named O'Domhnallain were surprised to find her alive. The woman—"

"Do you know her name?" Angel interrupted.

He whizzed past an arcade. The harsh rattle of machine-gun fire and sizzling laser beams echoed out the open door.

"Moira," Bascomb said, "Moira O'Braonain."

"Sorrow," Angel said softly, and the irony of it made him smile.

"Pardon?" Bascomb said.

"The name O'Braonain," Angel said. "It translates to 'sorrow.' "

"I see. Well it's a very fitting name as it turns out. Moira O'Braonain was thought killed in a tavern brawl in Clifden, Ireland, against a group of vampires only a few days later."

Angel remembered, seeing Darla point the long-barreled pistol at the swordswoman's face and pull the trigger, the sudden sprawling fall the swordswoman had made as she dropped backward. "Only she wasn't killed then, either."

"No. Later, she rode with O'Domhnallain when

his group of warriors overtook the vampire band they'd been pursuing outside of the city and put them to death."

So Darius and his people had been killed. Angel considered the information.

"It was only a few years later that the Blood Cadre officially banned her from their ranks," Bascomb continued. "She'd become obsessed by one vampire she insisted had escaped their efforts in Galway. Forty years later, when one of the Blood Cadre ran into her somewhere in Europe— they're not very precise with their data here because they were already trying to cover the story up—they realized that she was no longer among the living."

"What was she?"

"I don't know. I do believe she wasn't a vampire, though, because she's been seen in daylight. There's something else I must tell you, Angel."

Chafing on the inside to get moving, remembering that he'd left Cordelia with Whitney, Angel waited.

"That symbol Doyle drew and faxed to me," Bascomb said, "has a history other than with the Blood Cadre. It has been found at the scene of several rather gruesome murders over the last two hundred years. All of the victims were male. The records in the Blood Cadre files indicate that whatever is inhabiting Moira O'Braonain has a real grudge against men."

"I'll get the money I owe you for the research by the end of the week." Angel hung up. He placed another call, dialing the number from memory. He passed through the police switchboard quickly, getting to the Homicide Division.

"Lockley," Kate Lockley answered in a tired voice.

"It's Angel."

Kate was quiet for a moment. "You're calling from a cell phone?"

The question caused Angel to pause. He marked the time in his mind. "With you asking me that, I assume someone is looking for me."

"They want to see your client," Kate replied. "There are some questions the homicide detectives want to ask her."

"She's not ready to be interviewed, and it wouldn't be safe."

"The LAPD can make her safe."

"No," Angel said quietly. "Did you run her background check?"

Kate hesitated. "It's all false," Kate said. "Schend and his PR people reinvented Whitney Tyler to the point that most media people would never have penetrated the different layers of background, but we did. Once we got past it, tearing her last identity apart was even easier. The guys in

Forgery say it's some of the most detailed and best they've ever seen."

"Did you find anything?"

"Nothing." Lockley hesitated.

"What?" Angel asked.

"We got a hit on the symbol that we found at Whitney Tyler's apartment. It was in an FBI VICAP database. The symbol has been found at murder scenes for the last fifty years."

Angel didn't say anything.

"Doesn't that surprise you?" Lockley asked.

"Yes."

"Well, don't you have something to say?"

"If I did, I would."

"You need to bring her in, Angel."

"I can't."

"You're way over the line," Kate pointed out. "You're an unlicensed private investigator and now you're harboring a murder suspect."

"A murder suspect? For murders committed over fifty years ago? C'mon."

"The homicide people want to talk to her."

"Now isn't a good time."

"What if she kills you, Angel?"

"That's not going to happen. She's not a killer."

"There are people who know her who don't think that's true."

"She's innocent, Kate," Angel said.

"Whitney Tyler killed her driver." Kate spoke with confidence. "I helped work that scene. Forensics found skin and blood under the dead man's fingernails. He fought whoever tore his throat out. They'll make the DNA match with the tissue and blood. Also, while we were taking statements from the television crew, several of them mentioned seeing scratches on Whitney."

"Whitney just avoided getting run down."

"He'd been dead for a couple hours before you found him," Kate said.

"She was with the television crew all afternoon and evening," Angel argued.

"We're questioning the crew now," Kate said. "Everyone agrees that there was enough confusion on the set that Whitney could have slipped away the couple minutes it took to kill the driver."

"And not get blood on herself?"

"She could have been prepared for that. Let the DNA test prove us wrong."

"No."

"Bring her in," Kate urged. "Let her make her statement. It's really the best thing you could do."

Angel remembered how Whitney had been the night before in his apartment, how scared and vulnerable she'd been. And in his heart, down deep where his soul lived, he knew she was innocent. At least, part of her was innocent, the human part that he believed was still Whitney Tyler. The other part was—or belonged—to something else, something demonic. It was that thing that had committed all the murders that had been done. There was just no way to prove it.

Images of the swordswoman flashed through his mind again. She'd stood on *Handsome Jack*'s deck with her sword in her fist, so cocky, so confident of herself. So prideful. And Angel knew what too much pride could do to a person.

A stop sign forced Angel to brake suddenly.

"I've got to go," he said.

"Angel," Kate said, "they've got a strong case against Whitney. If you help her elude arrest, they'll bring you down, too."

"I'll have to take that chance," Angel said. "She's not guilty of killing anyone."

"She did it," Kate said. "Don't run. Have her get a good lawyer. She has the money, and if she handles it right, there could be a lot of public sympathy. Those attacks against her—"

"Will go on if she turns herself in," Angel said. "She can't come in. Not until that threat goes away." He hung up before the detective could protest. He glanced at the dashboard clock, watching time slip away from him, knowing he had only hours before dawn, before it was too late for any kind of redemption.

❖   ❖   ❖

Less than forty minutes later Angel and Doyle stood in front of the motel room door where Gannon was staying.

"So Schend was giving Whitney up to these guys?" Doyle whispered.

Angel nodded. "Hit show or no hit show, Schend's into the loan sharks in a big way. Including Yuan. An insurance payoff would come more quickly than residuals from the show. Maybe he was thinking he could replace Whitney without a problem, too."

"Man, that's cold-blooded."

Voices sounded on the other side of the motel room door, growing closer. Then bolts shot from inside. After Doyle had explained finding the man, Angel hadn't figured the Blood Cadre members would be in for the night.

"Ready?" Angel asked, dropping into a crouch.

Doyle gave him a short nod, setting himself.

The door opened and two men stepped out of the room into the shadows wreathing the motor court.

Angel stepped across the distance quickly. The motel was strictly low-rent so there was little chance of the staff calling to police, and even less of the police to respond in a timely manner.

The young man reacted first, throwing himself at Angel, not bothering to retreat to the safety of the room.

Fired by the anger and determination that filled him, Angel caught the man by the throat and clamped down, choking the man to his knees, then dragging him over to Gannon's side, knocking the man down.

The young man managed to hit Angel a half-dozen times, but Angel ignored the attack. Then he felt the man go limp in his grasp, passed out from lack of oxygen.

Angel opened his hand and released the unconscious man. He fixed his gaze on Gannon. "Get up."

"Or what, Angelus? You'll kill me?" Gannon remained calm. "I'm not afraid to die."

"Maybe not, but I'm willing to bet it's not something you're looking forward to, either." Angel took a deep breath. "I won't kill you, but there's a lot you can do to someone before you get to that point."

Reluctantly Gannon got up. "Where are we going?"

Angel pulled his car behind the warehouse he'd chosen as their temporary headquarters. He'd done some work for the owner in the last few weeks, getting the man out of trouble with a demon that had been trying to set up a black market ring.

Taking Gannon by the arm, Angel pulled the

man up the short flight of stairs that led to the loading door. He dragged the swipe card through the reader, and the door unlocked with the sound of a pistol shot.

"Why are you doing this?" Gannon asked Angel.

"Because you people stopped looking at Moira O'Braonain as a person long before you were born," Angel snapped as he led the man through the aisles between the warehouses.

"She's not human," Gannon said.

"And she's not totally evil the way you make her out to be," Angel argued.

"Do you know what she is?" Gannon asked.

"Not completely," Angel admitted, "but I have a good idea. She's been possessed by something. I want you to help me free her."

"Free her?" Gannon shook his head. "There's nothing left to free."

Pushed past all tolerance, Angel grabbed the Blood Cadre warrior by his shirt and pinned him up against a stack of crates. Before he could stop it, his face morphed, letting the dark hunger show. He saw the fear in Gannon's eyes, smelled it on the man.

"There's an innocence about her," Angel insisted.

Doyle put a hand on Angel's shoulder. "Take it back about a notch or two."

Struggling, Angel managed to cage the hunger

for the moment. "You don't know what it's like being trapped somewhere between good and evil, Gannon. Being raised up the way you were, dedicated to the principles you were given, how many real choices have you had to make in your life?"

"Becoming what she is was by her own choice," Gannon argued. "She should have died the first time you killed her. But she didn't. That was her choice. She leaned into evil's embrace, and it willingly took her. Do you know how many men she's killed over the last two and a half centuries?"

"Dozens," Angel replied. "I know. But that was the evil working within her. Not the part of her I sensed." He paused, feeling the ache in his stilled heart. "I wish I could make you listen."

"I am listening, Angel, and what I'm hearing is the guilt that you've taken upon yourself for your part in her death." Gannon shook his head, looking amazed. "Never did I think I would hear such emotion from a vampire. Where you live must be purgatory."

"It is," Angel said.

"So you think the salvation of Moira O'Braonain is going to put you further along the path to righteousness. Is that what this is about, Angel? Increasing your chances to get back to that life that you almost had?"

"I work to help the people I can help here

because it means something to me," Angel said, "and because that makes me think that I mean something in turn. I've seen a lot of people in trouble. Moira O'Braonain is one of them. I can't turn away from that. And I don't see how you can."

"What do you think I can do that you can't?" Gannon asked.

"You're a priest besides being a warrior," Angel said. "You can exorcise the demon that's holding her."

Gannon was silent for a moment. "We have thought about that in the past. We could also destroy her in the process," he pointed out. "At least, if we killed her body, her soul would be free from the thing that binds her."

Angel nodded. "She has to be stopped, no matter what the loss. I know that." He'd seen the love in Buffy's eyes when she'd pierced him with the sword and sent him screaming to hell. Other than walking away from each other after the Sunnydale High graduation, it had been the hardest thing either of them had been called on to do. "But I think we can save her."

"This is a fool's errand," Gannon said. "You could end up getting us all killed for you own selfish desires."

"That's not what this is about."

"Your guilts and conceits, then."

"We're here," Angel said, "because I think we can make a difference."

Gannon studied him for a moment. Angel saw the change in the man's eyes. "I'll need some things if we're going to do this properly."

"I've already got them," Angel said. He led the way to the office, where he'd left Cordelia and Whitney.

"It's about time you got back," Cordelia said in exasperation. She pointed at the small black-and-white television on the cluttered desk. "Did you know the LAPD has put out an APB on Whitney? There are people who believe she killed the driver and maybe the security guard in her apartment."

"She did kill them," Angel said, knowing Doyle was as relieved as he was that Cordelia was okay.

The office was a twelve-foot by twelve-foot square crammed with filing cabinets, the desk and computer, and a couch along the back wall. Whitney slept on the couch, looking little-girl small wrapped in an afghan. She was pale and slept restlessly.

"She killed those people?" Cordelia stood up from her chair. "And you left me here without telling me?"

"Would you have stayed if I'd told you?" Angel asked, lifting Whitney from the couch.

"No way. We're going to have to do a little

rethinking on this partnership thing we've got going." Cordelia followed him out into the warehouse. "Leaving me in the dark is not acceptable."

Angel placed Whitney on the warehouse floor, pulling the afghan tight around her. "I had things I needed to do."

"And if you'd come back and I was dead? Ripped to pieces or hanging from the nearest—" Cordelia looked up—"metal thingy?"

"I'd have felt bad," Angel assured her. He took the box Doyle had carried in, dropping to his knees and shaking the contents out onto the pavement.

"That's not good enough," Cordelia said.

Angel hesitated, knowing it was hard for Cordelia to actually see that they had other problems at the moment. He looked at her. "I'd have felt really bad. Probably the most bad I've ever felt."

Cordelia smiled. "You mean that, don't you?"

Angel nodded. "Yeah. But I knew she wasn't going to wake up with all the sedative I put in her coffee."

The smile faded from Cordelia's face. "There was no threat?"

"Not really."

"Then I didn't even have to sit in this creepy place all by myself. We could have left Whitney here."

"I'd rather we didn't do that," Angel said. "In case I was wrong." He saw the look on Cordelia's face again. "But if I'd been wrong, I'd have really, really felt bad."

All business now, Gannon joined Angel. "We're going to need to draw a circle of protection," the Blood Cadre warrior said.

"Yes." Angel pulled on a pair of gloves to work with the blessed chalk and drew the circle, then placed candles at five points.

"I don't like working in chalk," Gannon said. "If you accidentally break the lines or symbols, you unleash everything you're trying to hold in." He drew steadily, walking on his knees, using the flat side of the green chalk to make arcane symbols around the ten-foot circle. "I prefer paint."

"I didn't have any blessed paint," Angel said, starting the first of the nine binding words of power that had to be written around the circle, following after Gannon.

"The candles are blessed, too?" Gannon asked.

"Yes."

Gannon finished the circle, then started drawing the symbols along the outer edge. "By rights, you shouldn't even be able to handle these materials."

"I'm not like any other vampire out there," Angel said.

"I'm beginning to truly understand that."

Whitney stirred restlessly in the circle's center.

"She's not going to continue to sleep for long," Doyle said. "This spell you're setting up is beginning to take effect."

Angel knew that was true. He could feel the energy building himself. But he took his time, making sure that all the symbols were right. If they weren't, the circle would never hold the demon that possessed Whitney, and they were all at risk.

"You have holy water?" Gannon asked. "And a Bible?"

Doyle handed the man the Bible and the shaker of holy water. "If you have to use the holy water," he told Gannon, "try to remember that it can hurt Angel, too."

Gannon nodded. "I think we're ready."

Whitney moaned and opened her eyes. She looked at Angel and Gannon as they stood.

"We're going to have to be," Angel said.

"Angel," Whitney said, looking around in confusion. "What are you doing?"

"What needs to be done," Angel replied calmly. "What I can do to rectify a wrong I made all those years ago."

Whitney's eyes blazed with insane otherworldly fury.

"What is that thing?" Cordelia whispered, taking a quick step back.

"A banshee," Angel said, as he tried to figure out what to do. Somehow, he had to reach the innocent part of the woman the creature had cadged away.

"A faery thing, right?" Cordelia asked.

"Maybe," Angel said. "Banshees are of Celtic origin, but their actual beginnings are lost in myth. Or maybe they're all true. Besides the faery connection, they're also thought to be ghosts of unbaptized children, devils who wail for the souls that escape them, and ancestral spirits who appear before a death to start the newly departed soul on its journey."

"Wouldn't knowing what a banshee was exactly help?"

"I don't know," Angel said. "I'm working on the fact that she was once Moira O'Braonain."

Cordelia looked confused. "And she was?"

"A woman I killed," Angel answered, "over two hundred years ago."

"And she murdered those other people you're talking about?"

Angel shook his head. "No. She's innocent of that. The banshee takes over Whitney's mind at those times, the same as she's doing now. Whitney never remembers any of it. She also doesn't remember being anything more than human. With the possession, Whitney only remembers one life at a time."

Gannon opened the Bible and began to read. "In the name of the Father, and of the Son, and of the Holy Ghost. Amen. Most glorious Prince of the Heavenly Armies, Saint Michael the Archangel, defend us in our battle against principalities and powers, against the rulers of this world of darkness, against the spirits of wickedness in the high places."

As Angel watched, a glowing green barrier rose from the chalk to form a hemisphere that surrounded Whitney.

"What are you doing?"

"Come to the assistance of men whom God has created in His likeness," Gannon continued in a steady voice that grew more powerful, "and whom He has redeemed at a great price from the tyranny of the devil."

Whitney stretched a hand out and touched the green glowing barrier. Sparks shot out in a blaze of fire. She jerked her hand back in pain. "No," she whispered. She gazed fearfully at the glowing hemisphere. "You can't do this to me."

Gannon continued, his words rolling through the warehouse.

"Stop it!" Whitney slammed a fist against the

glowing wall, showering the interior of the hemisphere with bright lime-green sparks. The glowing wall grew more opaque.

Without warning, Whitney doubled over and sank to her knees. She sobbed in pain, holding her hands pressed against her ears. "You don't know what you're doing! You're going to let it out!"

"God arises," Gannon read, "His enemies are scattered and those who hate Him flee before Him. As smoke is driven away, so are they driven; as wax melts before the fire, so the wicked perish at the presence of God."

"No!" Whitney shouted, leaping to her feet. "Stop! Please!"

Gannon lifted his cross and continued relentlessly. "Behold the Cross of the Lord, flee bands of enemies."

Whitney doubled over again, her screams echoing through the cavernous warehouse. She morphed, changing into a bent, arthritic old woman with gray hair. Her bilious gray-green eyes focused on Angel, and she flung herself at the green glowing barrier.

Sparks filled the hemisphere with the intensity of a lightning strike, followed immediately by the booming crack of thunder.

CHAPTER SEVENTEEN

Incredibly, the green glowing hemisphere barrier held the trapped creature's wrath. The stick-like old woman hammered the dome with her fists, setting up a crescendo of explosions that reverberated in the warehouse.

Gannon, Doyle, and Cordelia drew back instinctively. Only Angel stood his ground, and the guilt within him held him like an anchor.

With a final shriek of frustration, she stopped her attack and glared at Angel. "I know you." Her voice was the creak of a mausoleum door opening for the first time in years, strong enough that it grated on Angel's ears and caused pain.

Gannon continued praying in a strong, loud voice that barely rose above the eldritch forces used to trap the ghost inside the dome.

"I want to speak with Moira O'Braonain," Angel demanded.

"Moira is dead," the old woman snarled accusingly. "You killed her, hellspawn. You broke her arm and left her to drown when *Handsome Jack* sank in those stormy waters."

"Yes," Angel said. Accepting his own responsibility for the deed was part of the price he had to pay. "Now I've come to save her."

"You can't." The old woman cackled insanely. "I already saved her. I reached out for her and breathed life back into her." She raked her curved claws against the dome.

"You doomed her," Angel said.

"Less so than you, hellspawn. I gave her life, eternal life."

"You killed in her name," Angel said. "She wouldn't have wanted that if she'd known."

"Don't be so sure." The old woman traced arcane patterns on the glowing wall. The patterns burned in little wisps, causing the wall to shimmer. "When I reached out to her in that cold brine, she took my gift willingly. I offered her the means to get revenge on the thing that had killed her. She was glad to have me."

"Then why lie to her about all the things you've done?" Angel challenged.

"She had no reason to know. She is still . . . weak."

Angel shook his head. "You haven't completely turned her. She's still an innocent."

Angrily the old woman lashed out at the glowing wall, battering it furiously, causing it to wobble and shift.

"Angel," Gannon said in a brittle voice. His face was covered with sweat. "I don't think this exorcism is going to vanquish her. She's too strong. It would be easier to destroy her."

"No," Angel snapped, turning to face the man. "We have a chance here."

Gannon looked at him. "You came to me because you thought I was the best chance you had at doing this. I'm telling you now, I can't do it."

The old woman cackled with insane glee. "The frailties of human flesh. Has it been so long for you, hellbeast, that you've forgotten? They are not as we." She spread her thin arms out. "We are eternal. Eternal in our hatred and in the bloodlust that possesses us."

"No," Angel told her. "Hatred and bloodlust are not eternal." He thought of Buffy, how he'd felt when he'd been with her, how he'd felt when he'd had to leave her. "I've learned some of the things that are. Belief is eternal."

"Belief is a lie," the old woman screamed, stringing smoky spittle across the inside of the dome. "It can't be weighed or measured."

"That's because nothing can hold it," Angel said. "Not even you. Moira was a believer. You haven't taken that away from her."

"She was a stupid, dead child when I found her," the old woman screeched. "Her pride and her fear of dying left her vulnerable to me. And I claimed her as my own." She turned her attention back to the prison that held her. Her claws darted out, testing every inch of the surface. Green sparks flared with every contact.

Gannon's voice rolled steadily in prayer, but it was failing. Doyle joined the man, sharing the Bible, lifting his song with Gannon's. The green glowing wall increased in brightness.

"You weren't the only one who killed Moira!" the banshee screeched in accusation. "The blond-haired woman with you that time in the Galway tavern shot her. I had to fix that as well. I restored her beauty. And there were still others. Men who threw themselves at her, who took advantage of her when there were more of them than she could handle even with her great skill."

"What about the others?" Angel asked. "Did all of them threaten Whitney?"

The banshee grinned, exploring her prison more, gaining confidence. "No. Not all of them. Some I fancied for myself. I've been killing men since before I melded myself to this little girl."

The words jarred Angel, making him remember a little more of the information he'd looked up earlier. "Banshees were also thought to come from the souls of women who committed the sin of pride." He looked at the old woman moving around inside the dome like a spider navigating its web. He remembered the swordswoman who'd faced him on *Handsome Jack*'s deck. "But that pride wasn't everything Moira was about, was it?"

"Don't be foolish, hellbeast. I am what's left of Moira."

"No," Angel said. "I've seen the real Moira." He remembered how she'd been on the ship, haughty and confident; but he'd taken that from her when he'd defeated her and broken her. Guilt swarmed over him, burying him for a moment.

The banshee pressed its withered face toward Angel. "She was not real. She was only a child, a proud, gifted child who believed in herself and her calling. You robbed her of that, Angelus. I gave her back strength and a purpose."

"To kill? That's no purpose. That's insanity."

"So high and mighty now, Angelus?"

"No. I'm just learning to be at peace with myself."

The banshee spun angrily at superhuman speed, the withered features turning into a blur. Her hands lashed out, scraping the sides of the dome, drawing lightning. Fractures appeared in the dome and the smooth outer surface took on a jagged texture.

"Angel!" Cordelia yelled, pointing up.

Craning his head, Angel stared up in time to watch an LAPD helicopter float slowly above the top of the warehouse, visible for a short time through the building's skylight. Even if the police officers aboard the ship hadn't spotted the green glow of the holy dome, they had a forward-looking infrared radar mounted under its belly. The FLIR communicated signals to an onboard monitor that would reveal anything inside the building above room temperature. They wouldn't read him and maybe not the banshee, but they would know Cordelia, Doyle, and Gannon were inside the building.

In the next minute the helicopter vanished, but Angel knew it wouldn't be long before the troops arrived.

"We can't hold the exorcism," Gannon said. "You'll have to destroy her if you don't want to see her go free."

Without a word Angel seized a short iron prybar from the top of a nearby crate.

The banshee stopped her twisting and spinning at once, focusing on Angel. She hissed and flicked her claws.

Steeling himself, Angel moved toward the dome, carefully avoiding the thick chalk line. He raised his free hand and placed it against the green glowing barrier.

The shock that resulted nearly numbed his arm, but his hand penetrated the barrier. Screaming, the banshee sped toward him, intending to take advantage of the break he'd created in the barrier.

Angel thrust his other hand forward, holding the prybar. "Iron," he growled. "If you've got any kind of faery heritage, you won't be able to survive it."

Stubbornly the banshee reached out to touch the prybar. As soon as the metal touched the wrinkled, sagging skin, the flesh blackened and the creature yowled louder than ever and snatched its hand back.

Even as the withered face contorted in pain and the banshee screamed, the features softened, returning to Moira O'Braonain's for a heartbeat.

"Angel," she gasped, and her voice was so soft that he almost didn't hear it even with his hyper senses.

More confident, but grimly aware that he was cutting down the options he had open to him, Angel shoved himself through the barrier. For a moment he felt certain the blistering agony was going to destroy him. Then he was through, unable to stand on legs that felt almost powerless. He collapsed.

The banshee's face was intact again in an eyeblink, withered features cruelly twisted. "Now you're going to die, hellbeast. You would have been better off staying out there with your friends." She shoved a hand out and pale blue lightning formed a sword shape. The blade flickered as if it was energized. She pressed the attack at once.

Rolling, feeling his strength coming back to him, Angel lifted the prybar and blocked the sword blow. An explosion of twisting orange and black flames flashed and faded quickly when the sword blade met the prybar.

The banshee drew back, gnashing its teeth.

Feeling stronger, Angel rolled to his feet. He gripped the prybar at the end like a short sword and stepped easily into a fencing stance.

With a shriek of maddened rage, the banshee swung its sword, cleaving at his head.

Angel blocked clumsily, his reflexes not quite back on-line after passing through the barrier that caged the banshee. He had to step back to disengage the magic blade. The banshee raked her claws at his eyes, and he turned just in time to let them slice his cheek instead of blinding him.

"You're an instant away from death, hellbeast!" the banshee roared with insane glee. "How does it feel?"

"You're too confident," Angel stated. He set himself in his stance again, mentally keeping note of where he stood in relationship to the creature and the wall. "If you had been able to kill me so easily, you'd have done it two days ago."

"She prevented me. I can only manifest when she sleeps. That night when she stayed with you, I waited for her to sleep. But she didn't. She fought me the whole time. She slept for a short time at the television site today, didn't she? And the chauffeur paid the price for that."

"You hoped I would keep the Blood Cadre from you until you could slip away."

"Lies!"

When the banshee attacked, Angel parried, slipping the lightning blade to one side, then he tried a tentative blow, instantly realizing that he'd pulled the blow too much to do anything with it. Before he could recover, the banshee cut him across the midsection.

Incredible agony burned through Angel, throwing his timing off. He stumbled, watching as Moira's face formed on the hag's body again.

"I'm sorry," she said in fear-filled pain. "I can't stop her."

"Yes you can," Angel said, breathing shallowly to block out some of the pain. "You're strong enough, Moira. You've held her back before."

Her face sank into the banshee's withered features like quicksand. "No, she's never been strong enough," The voice of the withered old crone insisted. The blade flashed again, seeking out flesh.

Angel blocked the blows, trying to ignore the pain that ripped across his stomach.

"When I first taught her to kill, she cried," the banshee said. "She had these lofty ideals, you see, that men had given her. I taught her to be a true female predator. We found men and we killed them. And every time we killed one, she could only think of you, how you'd beaten her and broken her on *Handsome Jack.*"

Angel whirled, moving the prybar steadily, getting the heft of it.

"After a while," the banshee said, "I made her start forgetting. It was easy; she didn't want to remember anyway. Then, when it came time to start looking older, before we overstayed our time and made others suspicious of us, I made her forget her past life and filled her in on her new one. I killed men, and each time I left a drawing of the Blood Cadre insignia. That was part of what drove them even further underground in the eighteen hundreds, drawing attention to them and their works as they searched for me. They betrayed her when they turned her away from them. It was the only true home she'd known." The creature leaned forward, slashing at Angel's knees.

Angel leaped, spinning over the blade. He landed on his feet and swept a backhanded blow out that caught the creature in the shoulder.

The banshee cried out again and wheeled away. Off-balance, it bounced up against the barrier, throwing sparks in all directions.

Squinting against the sudden blaze of light, Angel pressed his attack. The prybar wove an iron net before him, deflecting the banshee's attempts to penetrate. Doyle's and Gannon's voices sounded louder, stronger, and the barrier grew more opaque.

And in all that time LAPD forces had undoubtedly been getting closer.

"Moira," Angel called. "I know you're in there. You can fight this thing and take back your life."

The banshee cackled as it stepped back to avoid the whirling prybar. "She has no life without me, hellbeast, and she knows it."

"Is that right, Moira?" Angel demanded. He blocked another swing of the magic blade with the prybar, knocking orange flames in all directions.

"Yes!" the banshee screamed.

Too late Angel noticed the shadows creeping from the stacks of crates. Doyle and Cordelia were watching him, having no idea of the danger they were in.

He turned to show a warning, then the banshee knocked him flat. Evidently one or more of Gannon's team had managed to trail them to the warehouse.

The Blood Cadre members surged from the shadows, attacking at once. One of them knocked Cordelia to the ground before she could move. Doyle grappled with another, dodging the wicked knife the Cadre warrior carried. As a half-demon, Doyle was fair prey for them as well.

Two other warriors grabbed Gannon, yanking him down to the floor and pinning him.

"No!" Gannon cried. "You can't do this! We may be able to save her!" They didn't listen to him.

Without warning, the greenish dome exploded into a pyrotechnic blaze, like a soap bubble bursting. The banshee whirled madly, screaming with insane glee. Then she raced among the Cadre members, her claws flicking out and leaving wounded men in their wake.

Dazed, Angel pushed himself to his feet. He watched helplessly, thinking the Cadre warriors would destroy her at any moment.

The raucous laughter filled the warehouse. Warriors dropped as soon as she touched them, bleeding profusely. Some of them never moved again, or ever would.

Gannon screamed hoarsely, ordering his men away from him.

"Moira!" Angel bellowed.

The banshee halted for a moment. When she looked at him, her eyes held compassion. But that emotion was quickly covered over by inhuman coldness. "You won't reach her, hellbeast. She's safe with me now." She shook her head like an unhappy parent. "You tried to take something that belonged to me. Now I will take something that you seem to cherish." She reached out and snatched Cordelia from the floor.

"No!" Doyle cried hoarsely, batting a Cadre member from him.

Cordelia fought the banshee's grip but couldn't break it.

The banshee flew through the air over the crates, lifting Cordelia with her. "This one will make a fine new home for one of my sisters, hellbeast." She flew toward the front of the warehouse. "I will break her carefully, and wait until she is weak enough. Then, together we will return for you."

Angel sprinted forward. Cadre warriors challenged him immediately. He struck out mercilessly, chopping the men down as they faced him, leaving them bruised but alive. He vaulted to the top of the nearest crate, using his vampire strength to hurl himself out of the Cadre warriors' reach.

The banshee swept forward with inhuman speed. She gestured at the warehouse doors and they burst out of their moorings. *If the police weren't already interested in the warehouse,* Angel thought, *they will be now.*

The dock fronted the Santa Monica pier on the west. Piers ran out into the dark water. The banshee flew toward the ocean without hesitation.

Still holding onto the iron prybar, Angel ran after the creature. He watched Cordelia fighting against her captor but the banshee's strength was too much. When Angel reached the wooden pier stretching out toward the water, he heard two sets of feet slapping against the planks. He glanced over his shoulder and saw Doyle pacing him, drawing on his half-demon heritage.

"You get Cordelia," Angel said. "I'm going for the banshee."

"You may have to kill her to save Cordelia," Doyle said.

"I know." At the end of the pier, the banshee disappeared under the water. Angel and Doyle were only a couple steps behind. They threw themselves in and dived deeply.

Underwater, Angel could barely make out the banshee and Cordelia ahead. He swam, watching Cordelia struggling to get away. Kicking harder, he reached the creature with Doyle only a heartbeat behind him.

Angel held the iron prybar in his fist and rammed it into the banshee's arm.

The creature's mouth opened in a vengeful scream, but only bubbles escaped her lips. Blood stained the water.

Drawing the prybar back, Angel struck again. Doyle grabbed the banshee's arm that held Cordelia as the creature dived deeper. The iron burned the banshee again and again. Stubbornly she held on to her victim.

Then Doyle managed to break the banshee's grip and stripped Cordelia from the creature's hold. Holding on to Cordelia, the half-demon swam toward the surface.

Not needing to breathe, Angel swam after the banshee, finally managing to grab her blouse. He pulled himself down toward her, dodging the sharp talons easily because the water slowed the banshee down. Pulling himself against her back, he thrust the iron bar under the banshee's chin and pulled up.

The creature yowled in pain, silvery bubbles exploding from her lips and tracking immediately toward the sea surface, catching the fierce moonlight that burned down. She flailed again, trying desperately to get Angel from her back. Resolutely, he clung to her, holding the iron prybar against her throat. The contact hissed and sizzled audibly in the water.

Finally, the banshee stopped diving toward the

sea floor and rose up, following the pressure Angel used to guide her. They surfaced only a short distance from where Doyle held Cordelia, who still breathed deep, shuddering breaths.

"Moira," Angel called.

The banshee continued to scream and flailed out with a fistful of claws.

Angel twisted his head and let them go by, then levered the prybar more tightly under her chin, letting the creature know he wasn't about to let go. "Moira!" He gazed into the rolling, fear-maddened gray-green eyes.

The woman's face surfaced in the banshee's withered features again for a moment. "Angel, help me!" She looked scared and vulnerable, the same way she had that night in his home.

The sea splashed over Angel, filling him with the cold numbness. He focused, forcing himself to continue holding the creature. "Let her go," he ordered.

"Never!" the banshee shrilled. "She is mine! You are destroying her! I can't keep myself hidden from her any longer!"

"Nooooooo!" The cry that ripped through the air belonged to a human in pain, not the foul creature that had possessed her.

"She knows," the banshee snarled. "She knows what she has done. She knows about all the men we have killed together."

Desperate, Angel looked into Moira's gray-green eyes. "Moira, you can do this."

Whitney's features surfaced in the withered face again. "I'm a killer, Angel," the young woman said. "God forgive me, I remember them all. I even killed Tobin Calhoun and hung him from the suspended crosswalk before the movie was finished."

In the next instant the banshee's withered features leathered over again. "She is a killer! Would you doom her to know all the atrocities she's committed?"

"Moira," Angel called. "Come back to me. Don't hide from the pain. Heal it. You can do this. I promise. I'm doing it. God, it hurts, but it's better this way."

The banshee struggled in his grasp, almost dislodging him. "She doesn't want to hear you, hellspawn."

"That wasn't you," Angel said. "That was something else, something that wasn't you."

"No!" the human voice cried out.

"Yes," Angel insisted. "Yes, it was something else. Not you." He held the quivering old woman's body, feeling it shift beneath him, becoming firmer, more rounded, younger.

"I don't deserve to live." Tears streaked Moira's face. Her red-gold hair warred with the banshee's gray, flickering like a strobe light as the two personalities within her clashed.

"You do," Angel told her. "You've lived nothing of a life. You died too young to find out what you were put here to do. No one comes into this world without a plan."

"He's lying!" the banshee screamed. Her claws sawed into Angel's arms, attacking desperately. They submerged under the water for a moment. "Men lie! You know they lie!"

"Words, Angel," Moira said, gasping, spitting out water. "Those are just words. I've been tricked so many times before."

"It's no trick," Angel told her. "It's the truth. All you have to do is be brave enough to believe."

Moira twisted in his grasp, striving to elude his hold. Angel held her fiercely, aware of the police helicopter shining its lights across the dark, turbulent water. The Blood Cadre warriors powered a boat through the water toward them that they'd evidently taken from the pier. When they reached them, Angel was sure they'd show no mercy.

"I can't believe," she told him.

"Did you ever think that the man who first took your life would try to save it?" Angel demanded.

She shook her head, shaking in fear. She was staying in possession of her body longer than the banshee now. The iron prybar didn't burn her when she was Moira.

"Then believe in me," he told her in a choked voice. "For the moment believe in me, and I'll help you believe in the rest."

The banshee tried to assert itself once more, but Angel held on and clamped the iron bar tight. Moira reached up for him. There was a blinding explosion of green light, then the withered arm of the banshee became a young woman's arm that curled around the back of Angel's neck.

Angel dropped the prybar into the sea and wrapped both hands around her, pulling her close. He felt her shoulders shake as she cried. "It's okay," he told her. "I've got you."

"I hate to be the one to break up this little Kodak moment," Cordelia said, "but we're about to be invaded by the LAPD and the Cadre kooks."

Angel glanced up at Gannon, who stood in the bow of the powerboat. The warriors behind him all held weapons at the ready.

"It's over, Gannon," Angel said. "The banshee's gone."

Gannon peered intently at Moira in Angel's arms, then waved his men to put down their arms. He reached down and helped Angel pull her aboard.

"I didn't think you could do it," Gannon said honestly.

On board the powerboat Angel peeled off his coat and wrapped it around Moira. Even drenched, it blocked some of the chill wind that stirred restlessly over the sea.

"I had to," Angel said. "There was no other way." He glanced up at the sky and saw the police helicopter coming back around for another pass. "Time to go."

EPILOGUE

"I'm going to plead guilty, Angel."

Angel stared through the glass partition separating him from Moira O'Braonain in the visitor's cubicle in the women's section of the city jail. "I don't understand. I thought your lawyer was talking about basing a defense on temporary insanity. Gannon said his organization was going to pay the attorney's costs."

Moira was dressed in the orange jumpsuit all prisoners wore. Her red-gold hair was pulled back, and she wasn't wearing any makeup. Her natural beauty shone through, but she didn't look like the actress Whitney Tyler anymore. This woman was kinder and gentler.

The low rumble of other conversations around them was an undercurrent. The big jail guards were a reminder that there was no real freedom in this room.

"Do you know what options I have, Angel, even with a temporary insanity plea?" she asked.

"No." After Moira had insisted on turning herself in to the LAPD after they'd made their escape one step ahead of arriving police at the warehouse, Angel had felt completely lost. The justice system was so fickle.

"I can spend the rest of my life behind bars as a convicted murderess," Moira said, "or I can spend the rest of my life in a psychiatric ward in a padded cell."

"But if you fight this thing—"

"There's a penance to be paid, Angel," she told him. "You of all people should understand that."

"But you weren't yourself."

"And were you after you'd been sired?"

Angel looked into those gray-green eyes and knew he didn't have an answer.

"No," she told him. "I feel better about this. I couldn't survive in a psychiatric ward after everything I've been through. At least in prison, maybe I can help women who aren't going to be in all their lives, women who just need a little understanding and guidance to make it in the world the next time they get out. I can be that someone."

"I know, but it's so hard to think of you ending up this way. When I first realized that Whitney Tyler was really you, I didn't know how things were going to end up, but I never imagined this."

She smiled, and he found he enjoyed the softness and contentment in her face. "You mean after you'd saved me?"

"I wouldn't call this saving someone." Angel tried to keep his voice light, but it was hard.

"But you did. Living the way I was with the banshee was intolerable. Even in here I feel freer than I can ever remember."

He nodded, and wished he believed that.

"This will be a good life for me," Moira said. "I can make it that way. Before I was accepted into the Blood Cadre, I was going to be a nun. This won't be so very different than what I was planning."

"Back then," Angel said, with a small smile, "seeing you with a sword in your hand, I didn't get the nun possibility."

"I didn't see you as a protector, either. But here we are. In the middle of our redemption. I believe in an afterlife, Angel, and with the banshee gone, I can grow old again. I'll be free then."

One of the prison guards stepped forward. "It's time."

Moira nodded and turned back to face Angel. She pressed her palm against the glass.

Angel mirrored the movement, placing his palm out toward hers.

"When they send me away," Moira said, "I don't want to see you unless you're okay with this."

"All right."

"I mean it, Angel. Being in here, knowing you're out there helping the helpless, as Cordelia puts it, and being content serving your own penance, that'll help me be strong."

"I will come see you," Angel promised.

Her gray-green eyes sparkled, then she took her hand away and left through the door on the back wall.

Angel waited till she was gone. Then he took his hand from the glass and made his way back out into the dark evening that lay over his city. He found comfort in the shadows.

Despite how things had turned out, Moira was right in one regard. In trying to atone for all the things he'd done, he'd never expected a chance to help one of the victims he'd taken. He decided to feel good about that and let the rest of it take care of itself.

Doyle pulled up in Angel's convertible. "I was watching for you to come out. Thought maybe I'd save you a few steps."

Cordelia sat in the backseat, looking at him expectantly. "Well, are we talking about the groundhog-sees-his-shadow of major brooding sessions here?"

"Actually," Angel said, "I was thinking we'd hit a club I heard about this morning."

"Clubbing is good," Cordelia said brightly.

Angel slipped into the passenger seat and let Doyle drive. Doyle looked surprised. Letting Doyle drive wasn't always the safest of strategies. "I heard the place is being run by a couple demons who are kidnapping college students to sell as slaves."

"Oh, *work*," Cordelia said, sounding less perky.

"Well," Angel said, "there'll still be clubbing. And I tossed a couple axes and crossbows in the trunk."

Doyle pulled into the traffic, setting off a string of explosive honking and cursing. He tossed a hand up and waved. "I'll need you to go with me to see Yuan later this morning."

"I thought you took care of that," Angel said.

Doyle grimaced. "I did. There's just a couple wrinkles that need to be worked out."

"Do me a favor and tell me later," Angel said. "Right now, I need to get in a fight."

About the Author

Mel Odom lives in Moore, Oklahoma, with his wife, Sherry, and five children (Matt L., Matt D., Montana, Shiloh, and Chandler). He coaches football, baseball, and basketball, and spends every spare moment he has with his children. He's a big fan of the *Angel* show and doesn't miss a night! In addition to the *Angel* book, he's also written for *Buffy the Vampire Slayer, Sabrina the Teenage Witch, Young Hercules, The Secret World of Alex Mack,* and *The Journey of Allen Strange*. He's also done novelizations of *Sabrina Goes to Rome* and *Snowday*. If you like fantasy stories, he just completed the *Threat from the Sea* trilogy for TSR. When not with his children or writing, he can often be found on the Internet and can be reached at denimbyte@aol.com.

"Wish me monsters."

—Buffy, "Living Conditions"

Vampires, werewolves, witches, demons of nonspecific origin...

They're all here in this extensive guide to the monsters of *Buffy* and their mythological, literary, and cultural origins.

Includes interviews with the show's writers and creator Joss Whedon

Buffy the vampire slayer™

THE MONSTER BOOK

By
Christopher Golden
(co-author of THE WATCHER'S GUIDE)
Stephen R. Bissett
Thomas E. Sniegoski

FROM

POCKET BOOKS